KARGIL

A Saga of Sacrifice & Heroism

KARGIL

A Saga of Sacrifice & Heroism

RISHI RAJ

PRABHAT PAPERBACKS

Published by
PRABHAT PAPERBACKS
An imprint of Prabhat Prakashan Pvt. Ltd.
4/19 Asaf Ali Road,
New Delhi-110 002 (INDIA)
e-mail: prabhatbooks@gmail.com

ISBN 978-93-5521-478-2
KARGIL: A SAGA OF SACRIFICE & HEROISM
by Rishi Raj

Edition
First, 2023

Price
₹ 400 (Rupees Four Hundred only)

Printed at
Sanjay Printers, Sahibabad

This book is dedicated to the bravery of those 527 young men who sacrificed their lives for the pride of the nation during the Kargil War; we can never repay their debt.

The book is also a tribute to my father and guide,

Late Shri Ram Lal Rama Ji.

Testimonials

Our nation will always remain obliged and remember the ultimate sacrifice of the warriors who attained martyrdom in the Kargil War. This book will inspire the generations to come by making them aware of the courage and sacrifice made by our brave soldiers.

– Rajnath Singh
Raksha Mantri, Government of India

This book is worth reading since the author Rishi Raj personally travelled to those inaccessible peaks where the Kargil War was fought. The book being full of emotions is a true tribute to the martyrs of the Kargil War and is a must read for every youngster.

– Girdhari Lal Batra
Father of Captain Vikram Batra,
Param Vir Chakra, Kargil War

After reading the book, 'Kargil: A Saga of Sacrifice & Heroism' written by Shri Rishi Raj, the bravery of our son in the Kargil War martyr Captain Manoj Pandey once again made us proud. This book will surely inspire every youngster in India.

– Gopi Chand Pandey
Father of Captain Manoj Pandey,
Param Vir Chakra, Kargil War

Undoubtedly, this book is a true tribute to the Kargil martyrs. I thank the author for this great work and for travelling to all those places for threading the stories of the heroes in the form of a beautiful garland before us.

– Col. V N Thapar
Father of Captain Vijyant Thapar,
Vir Chakra, Kargil War

The book is priceless and will definitely inspire the coming generations of India as well as the World. This book should be kept in all schools, colleges, universities and also public libraries, so that more and more people become aware of the Indian Army and the real worth of our nation, INDIA.

– Meena Nayyar
Mother of Captain Anuj Nayyar,
Maha Vir Chakra, Kargil War

Message by Sh. Rajnath Singh

It is with immense pleasure to share that Shri Rishi Raj has authored the book titled 'Kargil: A Saga of Sacrifice & Heroism'.

The great heroes of the Kargil War have scripted the golden chapter with their valour, bravery and sacrifice in India's defence. The victory that the Indian Army gained in Kargil while facing hard and adverse circumstances is unprecedented.

The sacrifice of the heroes who laid down their lives during the Kargil War will be remembered by our grateful nation forever.

I hope this book would constantly keep reminding us of their sacrifices. Also, it would keep inspiring the upcoming generations by making them aware of the exemplary valour and sacrifice of our brave soldiers.

I, heartedly, congratulate Shri Rishi Raj for writing this book.

With best wishes,

–Rajnath Singh

Minister of Defence, Government of India

Message by Sh. Gopi Chand Pandey

A developing nation cannot forget the sacrifices of its martyrs. Just as the future generations need to be told about Lord Rama and Lord Krishna, it is equally essential to make them aware of the lives and valour of the immortal Indian martyrs and soldiers. This book 'Kargil: A Saga of Sacrifice & Heroism' testifies that Shri Rishi Raj, is fulfilling his duty by taking up the role of a true patriot quite responsibly.

While reading this book, the stories of the valour of Indian soldiers, made me reminiscence the memories of my son Captain Manoj Kumar Pandey, a Param Vir Chakra recipient and thus, rekindled a sense of pride.

Vivid portrayal of the sky touching peaks in Drās region of Kargil, extremely impassable areas of Batalik region (where Manoj laid down his life for the country), moments of extraordinary courage in adverse circumstances, fierce encounters, the strength of an Indian soldier to keep the pride of the nation foremost and unimaginable battle under strategic oddities, coupled with a collection of messages from the kins of the martyrs has, made this book a must-read for every Indian, especially the youth. Shri Rishi Raj personally visited me at my house. There is a deep sense of patriotism in his personality and perhaps that has been his motivation to pen this book. Else, why would anybody otherwise study the brave acts and life stories of the martyrs? I believe somewhere deep down in his heart, the life of a soldier and the feelings of a martyr, have made its own space.

Being the father of a martyr, I can understand the writing inspiration of Shri Rishi Raj. I would suggest him to write something on the issues being encountered by war veterans, brave women and specially abled soldiers in their day-to-day lives; that would help the society to sincerely appreciate the lives of the soldiers and their kins.

My infinite compliments to the book 'Kargil: A Saga of Sacrifice & Heroism'!

– Gopi Chand Pandey

Proud father of brave heart Captain Manoj Kumar Pandey, Param Vir Chakra

Foreword

That day of 12 December 1998 is still fresh in my mind when my son Saurabh Kalia was commissioned as Lieutenant Saurabh Kalia.Vijay (Saurabh's mother) and I were invited to Dehradun to witness the memorable event. The stars decorated on his shoulders bore testimony to his transformation into a disciplined soldier. But we did not realise that very soon, he would be laying down his life for the pride and honour of the Indian Army uniform that he was wearing.

Saurabh had always been passionate with a fire within to serve his country, India. When he returned home after completion of his training, he proudly handed over a cheque-book to his mother and told her to withdraw the desired amount whenever she feels like. Who would have thought 'that moment' would never come! Even today, we treasure that cheque-book as Saurabh's testament.

Pakistan did impose the Kargil War on us, but they would never forget the way our soldiers reciprocated them. Though, we did have to pay a heavy price for this i.e; the lives of our children. Nevertheless this pain and agony is unbearable, we hold our head high when we think that our children have contributed to retain the pride of our nation.

Saurabh and his five comrades were captured by the Pakistanis during the initial period of the Kargil War. They were subjected to grossly inhuman torture and later, their mutilated bodies were handed over to India. I was shocked to even think that people could treat fellow humans so badly, crossing all the limits of inhumanity. After all, the soldiers of the Pakistan Army are also human beings. Why this heart-wrenching ill-treatment then with my son and his fellow soldiers? This was point blank case of human rights violation and will remain so forever. I will always continue to fight against the country that perpetrated the maltreatment and its people who were involved in this heinous crime. This is not a trivial matter but is actually a direct violation of the Geneva Convention.

I remember, Saurabh had come home on vacation for a few days after passing out the parade ceremony of the Army. The feeling of being financially independent kept him top of the world. After spending around 15 days with us, he went back to the Regimental Centre of the 4th Battalion Jat Regiment. The 4th Battalion Jat is an extremely prestigious Regiment of the Indian Army and has a glorious past. We were confident that Saurabh would uphold the highest traditions of the Army with complete diligence and devotion. His words while leaving were, "Maa, you watch, someday I will do something extraordinary that will make me famous!" Late, in one of his letters which we received, he had written how proudly he shared with his unit, "Today, am proud to be a part of 4 Jat, but there will be a day when 4 Jat would be proud of me."

In April 1999, he informed us over phone that he was being deputed to some forward post. In the first week of June, my younger son somehow discovered that Saurabh and his five fellow soldiers were missing from the beginning of May itself. And finally, that ill-fated day of 9 June arrived when the Pakistan Army handed over six mutilated bodies to India at around 7:30 pm. They were later identified as Captain Saurabh Kalia, Riflemen Arjun Ram Baswana, Moola Ram Bidiyasar, Naresh Singh Sinsinwar, Bhanwar Lal Bageria and Bheekha Ram Moodh. Saurabh was just 22 years old then.

Just looking at the conditions of the bodies, one could easily guess the heights of inhumane torture made to these soldiers. Considering the seriousness of the situation, the then Chief of Army Staff General V P Malik requested the Indian Red Cross and the International Red Cross to conduct post-mortem on the bodies of these soldiers, so that we could bring the notorious act of Pakistan's in the world's eye. However, the Red Cross turned down the request of the Army. Jaswant Singh, the then Minister of Defence and an ex-Army personnel, also aggrieved by this incident and termed it as a crime against a civilised society. His mother, Vijay, was badly shattered by this incident and even suffered a heart attack. She could not even continue her government job post his death.

To secure justice for my son I struggled everywhere – within and outside the country; this continues even after 23 years and would continue till my last breath. It gives me a sense of content when I realize that even after 23 years of the Kargil War, people still visit us and talk about Saurabh with lot of pride and admiration. For sure, there is no pain greater than losing my son, Saurabh but his sacrifice has set a new example for this country and its people that they would never forget. When a common man becomes soldier, he dedicates his life to the nation not only to live but also to die for the pride of the country. Shri Rishi Raj, the author of this book, visited our house in April 2018. I learnt from him that he writes on soldiers and carries out the pious work of making common people aware of their acts of bravery. He has even travelled to Kargil twice. His present book 'Kargil: A Saga of Sacrifice & Heroism' is an attempt to make his readers aware how Pakistan betrayed India and forced this war on us and, how our brave hearted soldiers foiled the nefarious plot of Pakistan and reclaimed every inch of our motherland with dignity. This war is an example of the warfare skills, unparalleled courage and bravery of the Indian soldiers wherein 22 to 25 years old young soldiers willingly laid down their lives while discharging their duties.

This book sequentially chronicles the events of the war right from the strategic positioning to the victory of India, and the best part is that Rishi Raj Ji has written this book after visiting all those locations where the war was fought. This is certainly rare. This book would surely be a guide for the present generation. As far as I am concerned, I received full support from everybody; even the then Army Chief Gen Ved Prakash Malik had come to our house to pay his homage. But my incessant aim is still same for the last 22 years—to press the Indian government to take Pakistan to the International Court. My son belonged not only to me but also to entire country and the ill-treatment meted out to him & other soldiers is a blot on humanity; the culprits sitting in Pakistan must be punished for the same. Even today, I am fighting in the Supreme Court with the same plea. I keep receiving letters from almost all corners of the country, providing me silent support for this struggle. I will always be grateful to them and hope Captain Saurabh Kalia and his fellow soldiers will get justice one day.

– Dr. N. K. Kalia

Proud father, Captain Saurabh Kalia

❑

My Thoughts on this Book

Those who are young now, were certainly little when this war took place in year 1999. As they grew, they learnt about this war and its heroes, but perhaps not the way people in our generation have. We have observed and understood this war very closely and learnt about the lives of its heroes. When the Kargil War took place, I was around 24 years old, almost same as that of Captain Vikram Batra, Captain Manoj Pandey, Captain Saurabh Kalia, Captain Vijyant Thapar and other young soldiers who laid down their lives for the pride of Mother India.

During my schooling, I was an active member of the 6th Delhi Battalion of the National Cadet Corps. I even got opportunities to participate in many camps, fired rifles and also won the title of the best shooter. By the time I reached 10th standard, the willingness to be part of Indian Army was at its peak. In 1992, following the advice of my teacher at school I sat for the examination for Railway Vocational Course, but at that time I had only NDA i.e., National Defence Academy on my mind. I appeared for the railway examination thinking that this would help me to prepare for the NDA Exam that I wanted to take after two years. I took the railway examination and as luck had it, I cleared the same. I completed 11th and 12th standards at Railway centre itself. The Railways offered me a job immediately after completing my 12th standard exams. Everything happened so fast that my dream of joining forces got dwarfed in front of the basic necessities of life. I belong to a middle-class family and taking up a job was the call of the time as well as a compulsion. But I have never let my love for the forces and the country subside. The difference lies only in the fact that instead of a gun, my hand holds a pen that constantly keeps eulogising these patriots and will always do the same. I have already got opportunities to visit around two dozen border areas. It has become an inseparable part of my life to travel to the borders and interact with our soldiers. Besides writing on the real heroes i.e., the soldiers of our country, I also create videos on them to convey my thoughts subtly to the current young generations.

I am fortunate to make two trips to the border areas of Kargil (Drās, Batalik and Kaksar). These trips inspired me to write on Kargil. How our heroes didn't surrender even under terribly adverse circumstances and how they turned the tables on Pakistan who was assuming that they have already won it—all these stories of our heroes have been beautifully strung together in the book.

The Kargil War was straightaway a result of Pakistan's betrayal, though it also reflected the lack of coordination among our intelligence agencies. Quite unexpectedly, Pakistani forces stealthily occupied 150 posts located along the 160 km long Line of Control. Some signs of infiltration had already become visible long before this but we failed to make any definite assessment out of the same. However, all the nefarious designs of the enemy, though apparently looking unassailable, started falling like a house of cards in front of the distinguished tradition of the Indian Army and unflinching determination and valour of our brave hearted soldiers. Facing imminent defeat, the then Prime Minister of Pakistan started clamouring for help from his friends—China and United States of America. But this was definitely a victory of our political and diplomatic relations that both China and United States neither provided Pakistan any material help nor supported its action explicitly. This book sheds light on all these aspects also.

It took me around four years to complete this book. During the course, I had the pleasure of meeting a number of kins of the martyrs' families. I always believe that it is a supreme obligation for all of us to meet the families of those martyrs, interact with them to comprehend the lives of the heroes closely and express our gratefulness towards them. I often reiterate this at every platform—look for the house of a martyr around you and at least once in a year, make a visit to the family members to make them feel that the sacrifices made by their children have neither been forgotten by the country nor will ever be forgotten. This very feeling, and sentiment provides them self-confidence and self-contentment. After all, even those martyrs, while laying down their lives for the country, would have surely thought that their countrymen would keep their memories, their conviction and their distinguished legacy alive, and this thinking would keep inspiring our younger generations to serve their country.

For me, this book is an attempt to keep the memories of all those martyrs alive, and to tread the path shown by them.

Jai Hind!

– Rishi Raj

Acknowledgments

I wish to express my sincere gratitude to:

God and my Guru Sai Baba, who encouraged and inspired me to write this book.

My parents, who are the reason for my existence. My wife Sonia, who takes care of our home, our family during the periods of my travels; not only that, she is also my greatest critic as well as guide.

My lovely children Niyati and Kartikaye, who constantly keep me updated with the latest technologies.

My son Kartikaye Rishi, my niece Raavi Bajaj, and Nephew Shubham Pradeep who went through the first proof and offered some invaluable suggestions.

My brothers and sisters, who are my strength. My senior colleagues, who always provide their active support and keep motivating me to write.

My team members Paramjit, and especially Raksha Sharma, who helped me in completing this book.

My other colleague Shri Arun Sharma and his wife Smt Hitakshi Sharma, who arranged relevant published documents related to the Kargil War.

My several friends of Indian Army, who helped me in closely understanding the structure and operational processes of the Army.

All the family members of Kargil War martyrs, who spared their precious time and provided me an opportunity to comprehend the lives of these heroes more closely.

My childhood friend Gaurav Pathak and an old friend Mukesh Kumar, whose support made my Kargil trip possible in the year 2007 & 2018.

And special thanks to my friend and younger brother Colonel Prabhu, whose guidance was valuable for me.

Contents

1

Beginning of the Journey

Let's date back to the time, July 1999. I was a 24-year-old enthusiastic young man and despite knowing the fact of war between the two arch-rivals, India and Pakistan, I registered myself for the popular Amarnāth *yātrā*. The *yātrā* began on July 25th and fortunately, on the first day itself I got the *darshan* of Lord Amarnath, Shiva.

Parallelly, in June 1999 the Kargil War was at its peak. It was the first war in the Indian History, which Indians could watch in their homes on television; But this later proved to be expensive for us since we ignored the fact that the Pakistani nationals could also witness the same. Nevertheless, I loved hearing news about the war because of three primary reasons: First, I am an Indian, Second, Myself being an army aspirant, & Third, majority of the glorious army-men were around my age.

I would see a similar spirit like them in me, ready to lay my life for the sake of this transcendental land of Bhāratvarṣha, India.

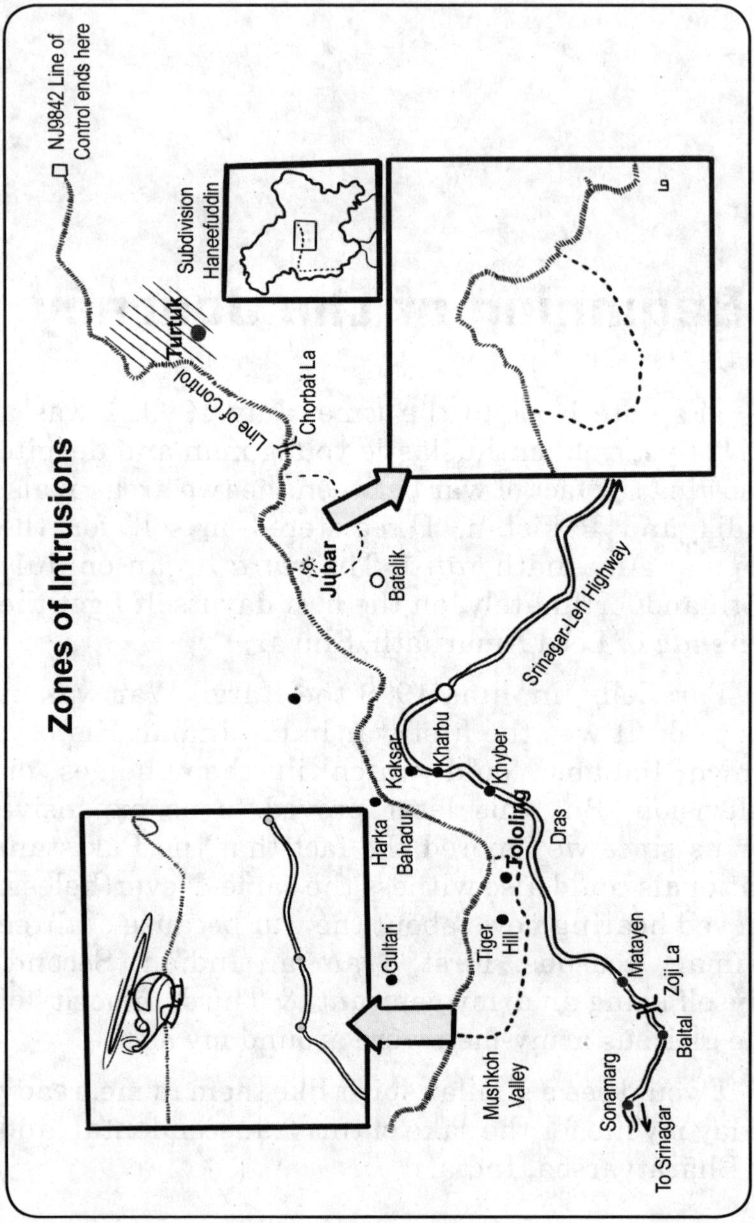

Map showing intrusions by Pakistan during the Kargil War in 1999

These youthful fighters had become the rising stars of India. Each and every family was coming to know their names. Unlike the fictional heroes of the silver screen, these were actual warriors. The list of such unparalleled men is unlimited, still if I can a name a few of them then they are, Capt Vikram Batra, Capt Manoj Kumar Pandey, Capt Anuj Nayyar, Capt Saurabh Kalia, Capt Vijyant Thapar, etc. This land of Bhārat has always been known for its bravehearts, and whenever it was required, they have come to the rescue.

It took us some time to understand that the Pakistani Govt. was then under the control of a military dictator, Gen Pervez Musharraf; but after some time, we smoothly controlled the situation. The Indian Army in a mere period of a few weeks, completely turned the tables and kicked Pakistan into the mouth of Satan.

My home is in Delhi, on the long Jammu-Srinagar-Kanyakumari highway. Very often, military vehicles would pass by on this very road. The look of the weapons installed overhead on the vehicles, was itself so fierce, then what could be commented of how strong our Army must be?

The vehicles would be carrying cannons and heavy arms along with ammunition. I still recall that every night I would pray to the Almighty to grant victory in India's favour, so that I could accomplish my trip to the Holy Amarnath Shrine without any hassle.

On July 22nd, I finally commenced my journey and reached Jammu the next morning by Puja

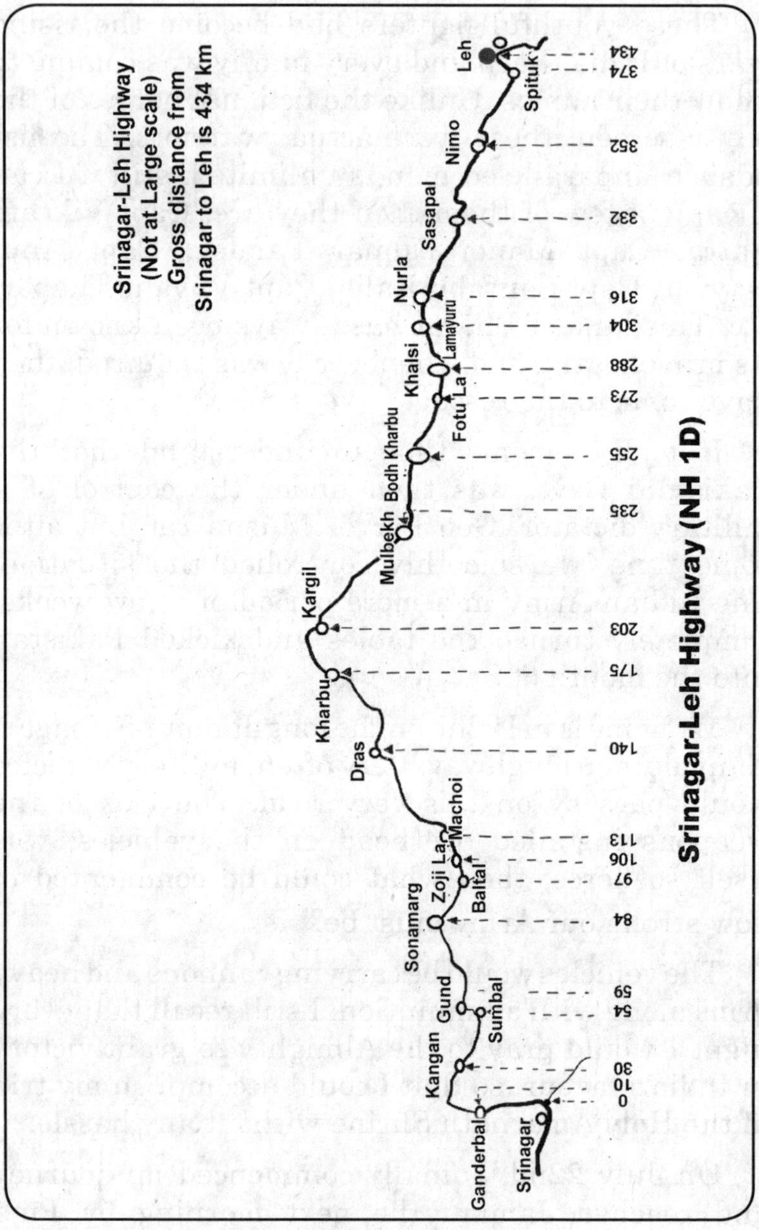
Srinagar-Leh Highway
(Not at Large scale)
Gross distance from
Srinagar to Leh is 434 km
Srinagar-Leh Highway (NH 1D)
Srinagar
Ganderbal
Kangan
Gund
Sumbal
Sonamarg
Baltal
Zoji La
Machoi
Dras
Kharbu
Kargil
Mulbekh
Bodh Kharbu
Fotu La
Khalsi
Lamayuru
Nurla
Sasapal
Nimo
Spituk
Leh
0
10
30
54
59
84
97
106
113
140
175
203
235
255
273
288
304
316
332
352
374
434

Express. At that point of time, there was practically no fear and I had no doubt since the Indian Army had pushed the Rangers back to Pakistan; because, an official end to the conflict was put on 26th July. Today, this day is celebrated as '*Kargil Vijay Diwas*', or Kargil Victory Day. After I arrived in Jammu, I collected some necessities from the local market for the yātrā. Our bus for the journey was to be taken from the Maulana Azad Stadium, at 5 am. Overnight, we stayed with our friend Arvind Sharma's cousin, Mr. Rajiv Badu. Next morning, we had to catch our bus at 4am.

Mr. Badu also got up early and dropped us at the bus stop in his *Maruti 800 car*. At last, my long-awaited dream was not far from reality. In my youthful years, I heard the song, *'Chalo Amarnath, Chalo Amarnath bhai ...'*. That always increased my excitement and enthusiasm. We took the bus trip to *Pahalgām, it was a part of a convoy which was heavily guarded by the Jawans of the Indian Army. Pahalgām is* a beautiful hill town, and gives a picturesque view of nature.

A major battle ground, in the 1999 War was *Drās,* which is located 64 km away from Kargil. Drās is located at a shorter distance of 48 km from *Bālṭāl*, another camp on the Amarnath trek. Even though some of my friends visited the battle ground, unfortunately I could not. I had taken a vow that once in my lifetime, I would visit Drās. Luckily, I visited the site twice, in 2007 and 2018.

On 22nd October, 2018, my flight landed at the Srinagar Airport. After this, we headed to Drās. After coming out of the airport, I directly went to visit the war memorial dedicated to the first recipient of Param Vir Chakra, Major Somnath Sharma. In 1947, the responsibility imposed for protection of Badgam Area and Srinagar Airfield, was on the shoulders of Maj Somnath Sharma. He performed his duty by displaying unparallel valour and leadership which resulted in successful safeguarding of this strategically significant area, in exchange for his life. For this valiant act, he was recognised and therefore, awarded the highest military war-time medal, the Param Vir Chakra.

Major Somnath Sharma

This glorious gentleman, even after losing a hand while playing hockey, sacrificed his life and performed his duty outstandingly well. Just some time before becoming a martyr, he wrote a letter, describing that the foe is just a mere fifty yards away from us; but we will not even move an inch back. That was his remarkable spirit.

After paying homage to Maj Somnath Sharma, we left for our destination, Drās. Drās is 150 km from Srinagar, which takes around five hours to reach by road. On the way, we also saw the stunning world famous Dal Lake.

In those days, the stone pelters were dominating the Kashmir valley. They were funded protesters by some envious political, religious and anti-national groups. Fortunately, those days are gone. At that time, no one could even imagine the removal of the controversial Article 370, which granted "special status" to Jammu and Kashmir. This article in the Indian Constitution, was continuously exploited to create divide between the residents of Jammu and Kashmir and other citizens of India.

But the good news is that under the Modi Government, the situation in Kashmir is improving and becoming more stable and the Article 370 has been invoked. Plenty of developmental works are now being initiated. At last, I wish the 500,000 Kashmiri Pandits, who had been forcefully thrown out of their own homes, return to Kashmir once again.

After taking pictures at Dal Lake, we bought some snacks, biscuits and few bottles of mineral water for our journey. The rows of Chinar trees on both sides of the road made us realise that we were passing through beautiful valleys of Kashmir. The air there appeared to have magic that infused a new life in our bodies, especially in our lungs. We soon reached Ganderbal. We saw some pushcarts loaded with fresh fruits and I felt a sudden urge to taste those juicy fruits, especially peaches and apples that were looking quite delicious. We got some fruits packed.

We do get these fruits in Delhi but they are not so juicy and fresh.

When terrorism was at its peak in the valley, the name of Ganderbal used to often come in news. Although, this was not the first time I was passing through this area, but this time we felt our heartbeats. I had crossed this place during my past visits during 1999 and 2007 also. Crossing this area after a gap of almost 11 years gave us a different kind of feeling.

My childhood friend named Vikram Vaid has few of his relatives who are Kashmiri Pandits. I remember having seen a lot of photographs of Kashmir in his house in my childhood. Though I was then a boy of merely ten years, those beautiful pictures of snow- covered peaks are still fresh in my memory. That time itself, I had made up my mind to visit and explore Kashmir at least once. I was fortunate enough to get this opportunity for the third time. I believe the number of tourists would multiply once the situation improves. Every Indian does have a longing desire to spend vacation in these beautiful valleys of Kashmir at least once in his/her lifetime. No idea why, but I feel myself to have some old connection with Kashmir. It is possibly because I am a Hindu and I belong to Kashyapa Gotra and Kashmir is believed to have got its name from Rishi Kashyapa. Sometime in the past, Kashmir was also known as the land of saints. Kashmir's famous litterateur 'Kalhana' has, in his book 'Rajatarangini' based on the history of Kashmir in 12th century, written the following lines about Kashmir:

> *"It is such a place where the sun shines mildly, it feels like that this place is created by Rishi Kashyapa, for his own glory. Residential schools, saffron, icy cool water and grapes rare in Heaven are plentiful here. Kailash is the best place in the three worlds (Trilok), Himalayas the best place in Kailash, and Kashmir the best place in Himalayas".*

That's why Kashmir is called 'the heaven on earth'.

This is the reason everybody gets dazzled for getting a glimpse of the natural beauty of Kashmir.

Just a little ahead of Ganderbal, we came across a river. And, as per my curious nature, I immediately asked Bhat, our driver, about its name. "Sindh", Bhat replied instantly. The Sindh River originates from the Machoi Glacier close to the eastern side of the Amarnath cave. It is just 108 km long. It joins the Jhelum River at Shadipora, 17 kilometres northwest of Srinagar. This very Jhelum River later enters Pakistan and joins the Chenab River in Jhung region of Pakistan. Further down, the Chenab joins the Indus River at Kot Mithan and this Indus River eventually flows into the Arabian Sea near Karachi. Hope you would have realised by now that the Sindh and the Indus are two separate rivers.

We had developed a good friendship with Bhat by now. There is no better guide than a driver for these kinds of trips and friendship helps in getting some valuable information in such a journey. Bhat told us that he belonged to a Muslim family but he also proudly shared that his ancestors were Hindus having surname as 'Bhatt'. Increase in Muslim population in Kashmir also led to religious conversions—Bhatt converting to Bhat and Dhar to Dar.

Moving ahead a little further, Bhat informed that we were crossing 'Kangan'. The road was quite smooth and the car was comfortably running at 80 kilometres per hour on that lonely road. Sonmarg was not very far from this place. We could view some snow-covered peaks now. We stopped our car again and quickly clicked some beautiful pictures. The Sindh River was running quite close to our road. Water in the Sindh River was crystal clear and cold. The flow of the river was fast and produced a melodious sound. That sound of water could be easily heard and sensed on this lonely road.

There came a bridge just before entering Sonmarg. The moment Butt saw that, he exclaimed, "Saheb, you would have seen this bridge in many films! Very recently, Shahrukh Khan and Katrina were here to shoot for their film 'Jab Tak Hai Jaan'." We reached Sonmarg and that meant we have already covered more than half of our route. Those snow-covered peaks at Sonmarg readily welcomed us with open arms. The sight of Dogri Panditji's vegetarian dhaba at once kindled our desire to eat and our appetite just doubled. We placed our order the moment we sat inside the dhaba. Sizzling rajma-rice along with tandoori rotis was more than enough to satisfy our appetite. The food was really delicious. I was just thinking, this spot might be definitely getting long queues during the Amarnath Yatrā.

Bhat expressed his desire to have tea, as if he wanted to get fully refreshed before traversing the snow-covered mountains of the Zoji La Pass or was thinking of getting rid of the sleepiness that was triggered by that heavy meal. Anyway, we all in fact wanted to have tea. PJ (Paramjit) asked the tea vendor to prepare strong and properly concocted tea. We decided to have a look at the valley for some time after finishing the tea. Gaurav and I got busy in reviving the memory of our 2007 trip here. During that trip, we had spent two nights in the Army Camp here and had taken the route from Sonmarg via Baltal for our darshan at Holy Shrine Amarnath. We were able to complete a round trip to Amarnath the same day through helicopter. We had taken rest overnight at Sonmarg again. Compared to our Amarnath Yatrā of 1999, the Yatrā that time was completed in a flash. Sonmarg bristles with activity during the period of the Amarnath Yatrā (that runs for almost two months every year normally during June-July). Vehicles full of Shiva devotees can be seen all around and holy chants of Shiva can be heard reverberating in the entire environment. Shiva devotees can be seen distributing langars at many places. For going from Sonmarg to Leh, one has to make his way via Baltal and cross the Zoji La Pass, that is one of the most challenging routes of India.

The Zoji La Pass is closed during winter because of heavy snowfall and generally remains open from June to October only. During the period of its opening, Sonmarg functions like an Army Camp. The Army uses that time to transport the entire year's necessary supply to the high altitude locations on the mountains of Kargil, Leh, Siachen and Karakoram. The time is very limited and the job is extremely challenging and tortuous. The Traffic Control Point (TCP) of the Army controls all the cavalcades going to Leh, Ladakh and Siachen here. During the months from June to October, entire Sonmarg remains jammed with trucks covered with green tarpaulins.

Zoji La Tunnel is being constructed here to facilitate smooth traffic towards Ladakh round the year. Once this tunnel is ready, we would be able to enter Ladakh any time during the year quite easily. Strategically, this project is very crucial. For some reasons, construction had stopped intermittently, but the work has been successfully assigned again by National Highways Authority of India (NHAI) to a new company with a hope now that this long-awaited project would soon get completed and we would be able to travel smoothly from Kashmir to Ladakh round the year. Completion of this project would also be beneficial for the tourists visiting Ladakh.

Exiting Sonmarg marks the end of the Kashmir valley and the beginning to Ladakh. Immediately after leaving Sonmarg, we were subjected to intensive security checks at the very first traffic point and then we proceeded towards Drās. It was just 20 minutes since we started, when I caught a glimpse of the Baltal helipad. It was quite deserted at that time. However, as I said earlier, we had used this very helipad to make that same day trip to holy shrine Amarnath in the year 2007. Recollecting those memories, we all performed chants of Lord Shiva and offered our respect to Amarnath from here itself.

Crossing the Zoji La Pass is considered to be a challenging task. A narrow road passing through ranges with snow-covered peaks all around makes this the most difficult route of India. This is just around 10 kilometres long but even this small stretch makes the best of drivers nervous. We also put our vehicle on this difficult road while chanting the name of God. Potholes and mud on the road and light drizzle from above—they all had made the condition a bit more awful, though unending picturesque scenes did make us forget all those challenges. We saw some vehicles parked at the roadside near the northern end of Zoji La. It appeared as if the area had experienced a snowfall just one or two days back. People could be seen out of their vehicles, busy taking pictures in the snow. Indeed, this whole view touched our hearts.

We also parked our car on the roadside and captured those aesthetic scenes. After spending sometime post enjoying the amazing sight of nature, we continued with our journey. A little ahead, there was a war memorial located on the left side of the road. This was built in honour of those soldiers who laid down their lives during Indo- Pak war of 1947-48. This place marked the end of Zoji La and thus, we entered 'Ghumri.'

The Indian Army celebrates 1st of November every year as 'Zoji La Day'. On this day, we had reclaimed Zoji La from Pakistan defeating their nefarious intentions. Pakistan was planning to capture Zoji La and also to detach Leh, Ladakh and Siachen from India. But, brave soldiers of the Indian Army had shattered the dreams of Pakistan. After the battle of India and Pakistan, the Zoji La Pass has been accorded a great strategic importance. The Indian Army had unexpectedly used tanks for the first time at such huge heights in this battle; this has not ever happened anywhere in the world till date. In the course of this fight, when Pakistani soldiers were refusing to withdraw from Zoji La, Lt Gen Cariappa devised a plan. Under the plan, tanks' parts were first dismantled and transported to Sonmarg by trucks. The parts were reassembled at Zoji La and the tanks were then used to

Field Marshal K.M. Cariappa

launch attack on the enemy soldiers. This plan of Lt Gen Cariappa was given shape by Brig Hiralal Atal. The enemy could not have imagined such an action even in their wildest dreams. With no holds barred, those tanks aimed at every spot of the enemy and compelled Pakistan to withdraw from strategically important regions namely, Zoji La, Drās and Kargil. Tanks were never used before at such altitudes anywhere in the world. This mission was executed secretively, trucks were covered with tarpaulin and all the areas that these trucks were expected to cross, had been placed under curfew to avoid the enemy getting any clue about it. Later on, when Pakistani army officials got to know about this exemplary plan, they found it hard to believe, as they knew that transporting tanks from Srinagar to Zoji La was simply impossible. But they did not have any inkling up to what extent the propositions of the heroes of the Indian Army could be.

Our brave soldiers not only created a robust blueprint for the same but also ensured its execution with all deftness. Eventually, the Indian Army was successful in driving off Pakistani infiltrators from Kargil and Drās. Who knew that we would have to face a similar situation again? In the year 1999, Pakistan re-infiltrated into our areas, captured our land, and managed to position their soldiers at our peaks which led to ***Kargil War***. The question now arises is what were the circumstances and motives of Pakistan that raged them to plot war against India?

❑

2
Anchor of the Kargil War

You might be aware that till date, India and Pakistan have fought four wars—in 1947, 1965, 1971 and 1999. Pakistan has faced humiliating defeat in all these wars. But still, no idea why, it ventures to initiate fight against India every now and then. The then Prime Minister of Pakistan Nawaz Sharif invited the then Prime Minister of India Atal Bihari Vajpayee, for a peace talk at Lahore in February 1999. The relationship between the two countries had gone from bad to worse after both of them conducted nuclear tests in the year 1998. PM Vajpayee always advocated peace and was in favour of a cordial and peaceful relationship between the two countries. On the other side of the border, Nawaz Sharif also wanted to bring peace through his democratically elected government. But, there was

Atal Bihari Vajpayee

someone who did not want all this to happen. A fire of revenge on India was burning in his heart for years and that person was none other than the then Pakistan Army Chief General Pervez Musharraf.

Facts reveal that Pakistan had already started working on the plot for Kargil incursion much earlier since the year 1987. Pakistan Army's pain over India's successful capture of the Siachen Glacier in 1984 and establishment of its sovereignty over the same had turned into a canker sore for them. General Pervez Musharraf is considered to be the main anchor of the Kargil War. He was the Brigade Commander at Siachen in 1984 and he was counted among the commanders close to the ruler Nawaz Sharif. Pakistan was badly hurt in the Siachen battle in 1984; while it was busy making plans, India established its domination over Siachen. Another pain that Pakistan was enduring for a long time was India's involvement in getting East Pakistan liberated from mainland Pakistan, leading to the creation of Bangladesh as an independent country. To add insult to injury, the Indian Army had taken 93000 Pakistani servicemen as Prisoners of War (POWs) and compelled Pakistan to surrender. This has such a great strategic significance in the military history of the world that Pakistan has not been able to forget its pain and agony till date.

The blueprint of the Kargil War was presented to every ruler who took over the reign of Pakistan after 1987 but all of them termed the plan as unrealistic citing their own reasons and the army never got the consent to go ahead with the same. Even some officers within the Pakistan Army, especially those who had participated in 1965 war, were always skeptical about the success of the planned incursion in Kargil. That war was also imposed on India by Pakistan and they had probably assumed that India, after losing the war with China in 1962, would be suffering a low morale and Nehru's death would have made it more vulnerable. Although, another reason for Pakistan's self-confidence was also the fact that it had superior military power and air defence at that time. Over and above that, open support from the United States of America was making those in power in Pakistan too egotistical. These misconceptions led Pakistan to venture into an armed conflict with India, the result of which we all are aware of! Despite adverse circumstances, India clean swept Pakistan in this war.

Pakistan army officials, who had witnessed action during those periods, were well aware that it was not easy to defeat India, irrespective of the strategy they used for the attack. But, there was something else in the mind of Pervez Musharraf. That was why Musharraf, along with his top commanders was missing when Nawaz Sharif and Vajpayee were shaking hands at Lahore.

In Pakistan, the army and the democratic government are two separate entities, each trying to preserve its dominance in all circumstances. Hence, it becomes quite necessary for each entity to maintain its relevance. For instance, if a democratically elected government of Pakistan is successful in improving its relationship with India, it will under shadow the working of Pakistan army and vice versa. This is the reason why Pakistan has always suffered from fraught civil-military relationship and many a times, the bitterness has unravelled in the open in the form of coups.

In the month of February 1999, prime minters of both the countries issued the Lahore Declaration according to which, both India and Pakistan reiterated their commitment to resolve their oldest issue i.e., the Kashmir conflict with all seriousness. It is said that for once, both Indian and Pakistan governments seemed to even agree on acceptance of the Line of Control as international boundary, putting an end to the long outstanding dispute. Pakistan army officials were concerned about this very possibility, as that would have forever brought an end to their existence as well as their power and relevance.

This is a bizarre coincidence that it was Nawaz Sharif who had appointed Musharraf as the Chief of Pakistan Army in the year 1998. Though, considering his seniority, Musharraf did not have any chance to become the Chief of Army, he managed to get the position due to his close relations with Nawaz Sharif. He had to overlook seniority of two senior-most army officers to elevate Musharraf to the post of Army Chief. At that time, he would not have thought even in his wildest dreams that the same person he was appointing as the Army Chief would one day dethrone him in future and mount himself as the head of the government of Pakistan.

For the smooth implementation of the plan, it was required to have trusted generals at crucial positions to ensure that Musharraf's instructions were followed verbatim. All such positions in the Army were identified and Musharraf deployed his most trusted lieutenants to these positions. The plan was already ready—it was now time to just execute the same. Musharraf issued orders to implement the plan with immediate effect. Everything was set in motion quite clandestinely.

In order to give shape to the Kargil plan, Musharraf had posted four of his most trusted lieutenants at specific positions; they were:

1. Lieutenant General Muhammad Aziz Khan
2. Lieutenant General Mahmood Ahmad
3. Major General Javed Hassan
4. Lieutenant General Taufiq Zia

Musharraf was born at Girdhari Lal Hospital, Ajmeri Gate in Delhi and he spent his childhood in Daryaganj. His family moved to Pakistan after partition. The Muslims who migrated from India are called Muhajirs in Pakistan and their loyalty to the country and the nation is always under the sight of suspicion. Hence, Musharraf might also be under pressure to do something momentous against India in order to get the stigma of being a Muhajir removed from his personality forever. Possibly, this was the reason why Musharraf was taking a personal interest in the Kargil infiltration plan. He wanted to devise an infallible plan that had no risk of failure. Several evidences indicate that the Pakistan Army had started deployment atop the mountain peaks of Kargil right from November 1998. They had started building bunkers that were strong enough to withstand bomb attacks.

Thus, by now you would have understood well as to why Musharraf could not have been a part of the summit at Lahore. *But this gives rise to a fiery question, that if Nawaz Sharif was aware of the machinations his Army was engaged in?* In the month of February 1999, when PM Vajpayee was pondering on the thought of peace at Lahore, many of Indian posts had already been occupied by Pakistan forces. Even a handwritten note was found on one of the rocks at Drās where a Pakistani soldier had registered his presence inscribing the date of 26th January 1999. In fact, diaries recovered from the dead bodies of many Pakistani soldiers also indicated that the Pakistani forces had not only infiltrated by January 1999 but also acclimatised themselves to the severe weather conditions there.

After the war, when the Indian forces settled down at those peaks, they were amazed to see the sangars there; sangars were found to have abundant food items like dry fruits, butter tins, biscuits and jams and even many bottles of wine.

The Pakistan forces managed to infiltrate and occupy 150 Indian posts built along the 160 kilometres long Line of Control, dodging the Indian Army and all our intelligence agencies.

By the month of April 1999, they had already built sturdy bunkers to stay; besides good amount of foodstuff, they had also stocked large quantities of arms and ammunition. They had made long term plans to stay in these bunkers.

Pakistan thought India would not dare to venture into a direct fight with them, as they would be positioned on top of those high peaks whereas the Indian forces would be placed at the bottom. And that would bring them to the negotiation table where Pakistan would demand Siachen in return for vacating these Indian posts. It is unfortunate that we could not notice any unreasonable activity there, even though Pakistan brazenly used helicopters to supply all the equipment, arms and ammunition and rations to these bunkers. Pakistan had code-named its Kargil operation as 'Koh-e-Paima' though some people also call the same as 'Operation Badr'.

After all, why are the high peaks of Drās so significant for both the countries? It is attributed to the fact that India's NH 1D Line of Control is just 8 kilometres away from this point and Pakistan could have severed India's link with Ladakh-Siachen by holding direct control over the road connecting Srinagar with Ladakh. This could have enabled Pakistan to have full control over Siachen. Pakistan thought that India would never like to lose such a strategically important region and would surely come to the negotiating table. Pakistan also thought that India would never venture to confront Pakistan face to face and that is where it made a mistake. Pervez Musharraf failed miserably in assessing the capability of Indian forces. He perhaps forgot his country's past. He forgot how Pakistan was battered by India in 1947-48, 1965 and 1971.

All these activities continued in a highly surreptitiously way until the beginning of May 1999. The Pakistan forces were quite elated, ready to fire on us after comfortably infiltrating our own border. In any case, it was supposed to come to light one day.

On 3rd May 1999, a local shepherd Tashi Namgyal from Gharkon in Batalik sector spotted some armed people on the Indian side of the border. He immediately reported the same to the Indian Army. The Army swiftly came into action. The very next day i.e., on 4th May, a patrol team was sent to scan the area, but it was fired upon from nearby peaks. Looking through their binoculars, our soldiers discovered that the attackers were dressed in black Pathani suits and were even equipped with radio sets for communication. Comprehending the seriousness of the situation, the Army deputed a new patrol team led by Captain Vikrant Desai on 6th May. Though this team could not meet the previous team who were sent earlier, yet Captain Vikrant Desai confirmed the presence of the enemy to his Commanding Officer. The Indian Army promptly came into action. On 9th of May, a new patrol team led by Captain Surrvey was sent there to assess the gravity of infiltration and another major action initiated was to rapidly deploy two regiments of the Indian Army—1/11 Gorkha Rifles and 12 Jammu & Kashmir Rifles, (who were on their way after completing their tenure in Siachen), to the Batalik sector.

❑

3

Beginning of the War

Once India got the slightest clue of infiltrations in May 1999, Pakistan started to play its cards and gave its signal for the beginning of the war. Pakistan found this time to be most favourable, because Zoji La Pass was still closed. Pakistan was confident that India would not be able to manage its supplies, if the attack was launched at this point of time. This entire theory was based on the perception that the Zoji La Pass which connects Kargil to India is usually opened in the last week of May. But, even luck was favouring India. On account of scanty snowfall during 1999, the Zoji La Pass was opened in the first week of May that year. The then Chief of the Army Staff Gen Ved Prakash Malik has described in his book 'Kargil: From Surprise to Victory' how Zoji La had provided its invaluable support to the Indian Army. We were able to transport 19000 tonnes of supplies to Drās, Kargil and other war zones crossing the Zoji La Pass under adverse conditions. Over all, the early opening of the Zoji La Pass badly ruined the evil intentions of Pakistan.

Intensity of shelling from the enemy side went up rapidly after 6th May. The main army ammunition depot at Kargil became the target of Pakistani bombardment on 9th May and we lost ammunitions valued in crores. This was a traumatic incident which deeply impacted our retaliation against Pakistan. Destruction of the ammunition depot was a strong signal to hard times ahead, though we could not figure out the same with required seriousness then. In view of heavy shelling from Pakistan's side, people in many towns of Drās, Kargil and Batalik were evacuated to other safe locations.

On 10th May, The then Chief of the Army Staff General V P Malik left for his pre-scheduled official tour of Poland and Czech Republic. Also, the Northern Commander of the Indian Army Lieutenant General Hari Mohan Khanna proceeded on leave. On 12th May, infiltrators were seen over Tololing peak. On 13th May, some more regiments of the Army namely 1 Naga and 8 Sikh were deployed in that zone.

By then Pakistan had started to target National Highway 1 openly. Initially it appeared to be a nuisance of some random infiltrators. Even some of our officials were taking these attacks lightly. But the kind of arms and ammunitions being used for those attacks indicated involvement of some trained army soldiers. By mid of May, the Indian Army sprang into action. But everything was still uncertain—when, what and how to retaliate? Even their exact locations could not be zoered down till now. But yes, to get our motherland evacuated from the infiltrators was certain.

It was crystal clear by now that it was Pakistan who had some ulterior motive to occupy the Indian land illegitimately. You may call this anything—a failure of our secret intelligence unit, or our fate—but it was now for us to face the results! We did not have any option except to challenge and annihilate the enemy who were occupying prominent positions over high peaks and to recapture each and every inch of our land.

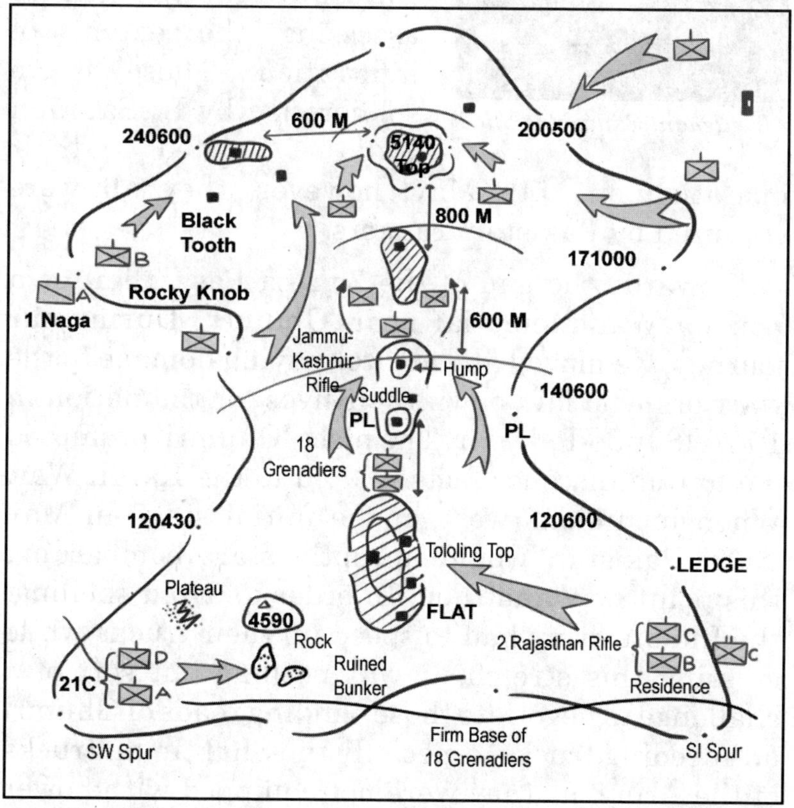

Map showing the operation of the Indian Army in Tololing Battlefield.

In the meanwhile, in order to get a clear picture of the situation, Lt Saurabh Kalia of 4 Jat Regiment, then manning Bajrang Post of Kaksar near Kargil, along with his five colleagues, Havildar Arjun Ram, Bhanwar Lal, Bhikha Ram, Moola Ram and Naresh Singh, was sent for assessing the extent of infiltration. These brave soldiers led by Lt Saurabh Kalia started their operation on 15th May; however, they all were captured by Pakistani rangers.

Lieutenant Saurabh Kalia

Towards the end of the Zoji La Pass, there is a Zoji La War Memorial near 'Ghumri'. During our journey, we moved ahead after paying homage to the warriors who laid down their lives for the nation in 1947-48 Indo-Pak war. The place 'Ghumri' prompted me to reminiscence facts related to the Kargil War. When incursions were in the initial stage in May 1999, Pakistan would abruptly start bombarding this point now and then. In order to avoid shelling, the Indian Army had to speed up their trucks while crossing this stretch. It was nothing but sort of a challenge to negotiate those winding roads of Ghumri on speeding trucks, especially the Shaktiman trucks of the Army, as they were not equipped with power steering then. They had to turn off the headlights of their trucks before entering that stretch, to prevent the enemy from catching their movement and launching attacks. Also, two soldiers holding torches would run ahead of the trucks and keep switching on and off their torches regularly; that helped them to avoid getting detected by the enemy and also prevent the trucks from falling into gorges. However, there were instances of the speeding trucks crashing against rocks or falling in gorges. Recovering them and getting them repaired used to be a big challenge for the Army engineers. While crossing the stretch that day, I was trying not only to reconstruct those scenes in my mind but also to perceive how challenging that job would have been. The Kargil War was fought mainly in Drās; beyond that, encounters also took place near Siachen Base camp in north and up to Ghumri in the south. Geographically, the war was fought on the heights right from Kaobal Gali up to Turtuk. In simple words, Pakistan had infiltrated around 160 Indian posts along 150 kilometres long Line of Control.

Just ahead of Ghumri, we reached a Police Post; this place is known as 'Mughalpura'.While coming out of Mughalpura, I noticed a board with the word 'Matayen' written over the same. During the war, it was the point 4875 that is now known as 'Batra Top'. It was the sight of a decisive battle fought from the Army base at Matayen. Good number of Bofors guns were deployed here. Beyond this point is located Pandrass, that is named after the Pandavas. It is said that there is also a Draupadi Kund nearby where Draupadi had once taken a bath. There is a peak here, that is believed to be scaled by nobody (except the Pandavas) till date. This entire region was targeted and heavily bombarded by the enemy during the war, which is why, there was always a fear of some bomb landing on the road there.

A little beyond this place we found the 'Batra Transit Camp'. We could see Point 4875 from there. Captain Vikram Batra had laid down his life while trying to capture this very peak. Now, this transit camp and Point 4875 have been named after him as a token of tribute. Capturing Point 4875 was absolutely vital in this war, as the enemy was able to control around 20 kilometres of National Highway 1D from here.

Dusk was setting in. I looked at the watch; it was around 5 pm. It was a cold evening. I got out of the car and put on my jacket. After a 10-minute break here, we straightaway headed to Drās. Our stay here was arranged in the rest house of the Headquarters of 5 Mountain Brigade.

Till May 1999, 121 (Independent) Infantry Brigade under 15 Core (Headquarters Srinagar) of the Northern Command was responsible for the security of Kargil-Drās region. But when the war entered into a critical phase and the Army was convinced that it was not a minor mujahideen operation (as it appeared to be in the beginning) but a big conspiracy of the Pakistan Army. Immediately, an additional division of the Indian Army was deployed there. For your information and to make it simple for you to understand the situation,

I am listing below the hierarchy of the army. This is based on the postings during the period from May 1999 to June 1999.

1.	**Chief of Army**	- General V. P. Malik
2.	**Northern Army Commander**	- Lt General Hari Mohan Khanna
3.	**Corps Commander**	- Lt General Krishna Pal
4.	**3rd Infantry Division Commander**	- Lt General Hari V. S. Budhwar
4.1	**8th Mountain Division Commander**	- Major General Mohindar Puri
5.	**121st (Independent) Infantry Brigade Commander**	- Brigadier Surender Singh (Until end of May 1999)
5.1	**56th Mountain Brigade Commander**	- Brigadier Amar Aul
5.2	**192nd Mountain Brigade Commander**	- Brigadier M. P. S Bajwa.

Usually there are 3 to 4 Battalions under a brigade; they are commanded by Colonel level officers. Until May 1999 i.e., until the start of the Kargil War, four Battalions and one paramilitary force coming under 121 Infantry Brigade were responsible for the security of Drās and Kargil.

1. **16 Grenadiers**—Drās
2. **4 Jat**—Kaksar

3. **10 Garhwal**—Indus
4. **3 Punjab**—Batalik
5. **8 BSF**—Channigund

The enemy soldiers were positioned at the top of the peaks and were in a better state than us. They had occupied their positions long back in extremely cold weather and hence did not require to get acclimatised. Moreover, they had all the stuff required to protect themselves from the harsh winters; they were also equipped with necessary arms and ammunitions. It is said that an enemy positioned above is 10 times more lethal than the opponent stationed below. Even a stone thrown from a height impacts like a bullet. This was the reason that the Indian Army deployed soldiers in the entire war zone in the ratio of 16:1 i.e., 16 Indian soldiers for every Pakistani soldier. Usually, this deployment is made in the ratio of 3:1. The Army had taken this decision in view of the inaccessible roads, unfavourable weather and the enemy having natural advantage of height; ultimately it proved to be quite supportive in winning the war.

We finally reached our guesthouse. We were welcomed with hot tea and warned that the temperature was going to fall below zero in the night. We felt a shiver on hearing this. The Reception Officer, in the course of his briefing, informed us that next morning he would show us all the important peaks, the names of which were on the fingertips of every Indian during the Kargil War. I had got this opportunity during my earlier trip in 2007, but this place was like the greatest pilgrimage site and there could never be enough visitation of the same. Now, in 2018, it felt like getting a chance to relive all those memories and clear remaining doubts pertaining to war. We went to our room and opened our bags. We had just freshened up and were thinking of taking some rest when we got the call from the mess. Paramjit and Mukesh were just too happy, as they were the only ones among the four of us who loved drinking. In that weather with temperature set to go below zero, rum or whisky is nothing short of a boon, especially, for people who drink. Both of them took full advantage of the opportunity and prepared themselves well to face the fury of the weather. As Gaurav and I do not drink, we relished the soup. Dinner was served around 8:30 pm and while having it, we got an opportunity to interact with some army officers deployed in the Drās region. After finishing our dinner, we straightaway returned to our room, as weather did not permit a stroll outside.

After getting into the room we turned on the heater first. The heater in the room seemed to be inadequate as it was getting colder gradually. At around 11 pm, we checked the temperature, and got shocked! The temperature was 10 degrees below zero and my phone indicated it was to go further below to -16 degrees by midnight. I immediately took a screen shot in my phone and forwarded the same to some of my friends. This was going to be the coldest night of my life. We somehow spent the night shivering

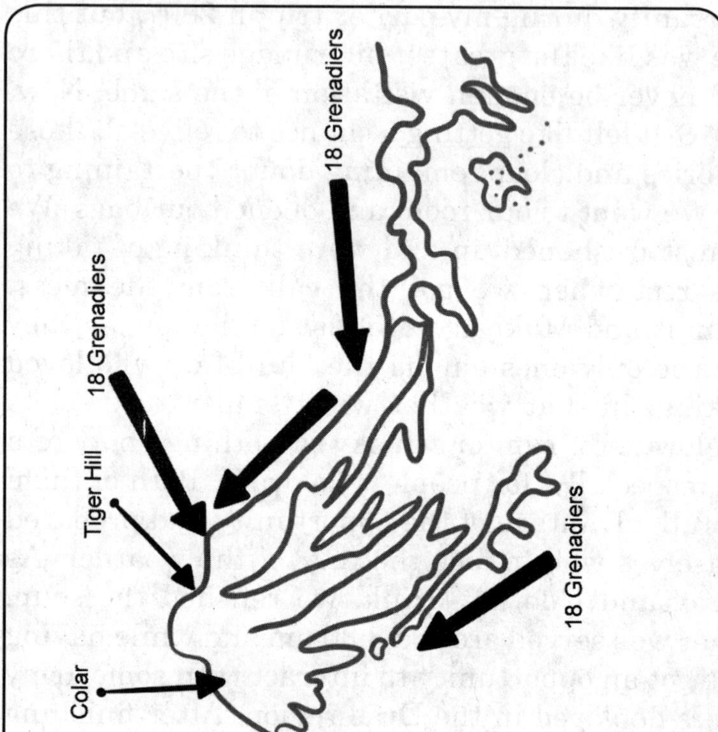

Map showing action taken by Indian Army on Tiger Hill

in cold and thus we decided to spend the next night at Kargil where the weather is comparatively less severe.

Drās is the world's second coldest inhabited place where temperature had once gone to 60 degrees below zero. It may not be wrong to call Drās, the Siberia of India. Located at an altitude of around 10,500 ft., Drās experiences bone-chilling cold weather. The peaks where the war was fought have still higher altitudes going up to 16,000 ft. Nowhere, in the world has a war been fought on barren mountains at such heights under icy winds (the temperature here had gone up to 16 degrees below zero during the war) where it is difficult to even find a place to hide. The enemy was able to directly fire at the soldiers who were trying to scale the heights; but those Indian soldiers were probably too valorous. The adverse conditions could neither unnerve them nor weaken their morale even a bit. Just in a few days, they successfully threw out the Pakistani forces out of the Indian border and showed them their right place.

The morning at Drās was quite pleasant. However, it was not a pleasing experience when it came to washrooms; as the water in the pipes were frozen! Even brushing our teeth was a daunting task. I just realised, if we had to face so many problems in a single day, what extent of suffering those soldiers endured on regular postings on a daily basis? Our heartfelt respect to all those soldiers for the kind of adverse conditions they had to bear during the Kargil War! Anyway, the issues were sorted out quickly and, after finishing our breakfast at the mess, we packed our bags and left to grasp the sight of the peaks which got famous during the war.

For me, this was going to be quite significant and memorable. I was planning to make use of every moment of the day. The first glimpse of sunshine broke the silence of darkness with clear weather.

Few of the peaks that had become eminent during the Kargil War seemed closer from the Brigade Command Headquarters. One soldier was deputed with us for the day.

At the brigade command military canteen, we bought balaclava (a special type of woolen cap generally used by soldiers). The weather was stunningly clear and the sun was shining brightly. The shining Tiger Hill was looking like a beautiful crown on the head of our Mother India. I remember very well that I witnessed a cloudy weather during my last trip in 2007 and I got the opportunity to go on top of the 'Sando Top' at that time. A board atop that peak is still fresh in my mind; it had explicit warning, "You are in the firing range of the enemy and a bullet may hit you any time."

Next, we were curious to see the Tiger Hill. Unfortunately, due to cloudy weather last time, even though we were standing just in front of the Tiger Hill it was hardly visible. This time perhaps it was a sign from the nature that with clear sunny weather we viewed all the peaks very clearly. I bought a balaclava for my father also. My father was very fond of caps and I was fond of travelling. I would never forget buying a cap for him whenever I visited a new place.

We all bought souvenirs and started for our next destination where we expected to get a clear view of the entire Drās area. It took around 20 minutes to reach that point which was approximately 10 Kms away from Drās. Our soldier guide apprised that we were lucky to have clear weather and we would be able to view all the peaks clearly.

The weather in Drās region is quite unpredictable and a good weather is rare. Fortune was in our favor with us that day. We were feeling elated. We were briefed about the peaks in detail. The Tiger Hill was right in front of us in all its grandeur. The wind was trying to make its way through our jackets but we were also prepared. Although there was no binoculars to view the peaks; however, the peaks were demonstrated in a clear and unique way. Subedar saheb explained the peaks by keeping some fingers of one hand over the other. For me, it was a bit easy, as I had gone to Sando Top last time; thus, that had made me somewhat familiar with the area. Now, we were standing at much higher altitude than that of the same Sando Top .

Here, we visited the point where Bofors guns were deployed to target the enemy directly. Bofors proved to be nothing less than a boon for us during the Kargil War. Our Kargil victory would have been quite difficult in the absence of these Bofors guns. We spent around one and a half hour at that location and attentively looked around and analysed every minute detail related to every peak that was critical during the war. While returning, we parked our car near Drās Nalah (In this region, a small river is referred to as Nalah). Witness to all the dismay of the war, this Drās Nalah was flowing in full swing that day also. Its cold and transparent water did deserve an *Aachaman (sip)*! This very Drās Nalah joins the Shingo River further down in Kaksar that comes from Pakistan. This Shingo River later joins the Suru River and then flows from Kargil into Skardu district. Immediately after crossing the Line of Control (LOC), Shingo joins the Indus River at a place known as 'Marol'. For the benefit of the readers, I would like to mention that this very Indus River flows through Batalik region in India before entering the Pakistan occupied Kashmir. Though, we did not feel like leaving the bank of the Drās Nalah, yet we proceeded to visit Kargil War Memorial. However, viewing the dominant peaks of the Drās area was indeed an inspiring and cherishing experience for us.

We soon arrived at the Kargil War Memorial. Just behind this memorial, The Tololing peak can be seen, which is a symbol of our pride, faith and courage. During the Kargil War, securing victory over Tololing was critical, as a major portion of the National Highway 1D came under the firing range of the enemy from this peak. LOC is just 8 kilometres away from the Tololing. The enemy soldiers' infiltration up to Tololing was a major challenge for us. I will talk about this in detail later. We had not been able to sleep well previous night due to severe cold. Hence, we chose Kargil for this night's stay; as cold is comparatively less severe here. All the information relating to the Kargil War has been provided in detail at the war memorial. Even the arms that were recovered from Pakistani infiltrators and soldiers have been put on display there. The identity cards also displayed that prove that those fighting the war were all Pakistan Army's regular soldiers. The memorial showcased evidence that showed how our soldiers had foiled the wicked plans of Pakistan with great courage and valour.

The gallery that houses these items has been named after Captain Manoj Kumar Pandey, Param Vir Chakra. The small helipad here has been named after Captain Vijyant Thapar. Firearms that were used in the Kargil War were also on display. The names of the martyrs have been engraved on brass plates with few lines of famous poems written by Makhan Lal Chaturvedi, which goes like this :-

Chah Nahin Mai SurBala Ke Gehnon Mein Guntha Jaaon.
Chah Nahin Premi Mala Mein Bindh, Pyari Ko Lalchaon.
Chah Nahin Samraton Ke Shav Par, He Hari Dala Jaaon.
Chah Nahin Devon Ke Sar Par Chadhon, Bhagya Par Itraoon.
Mujhey Tod Lena Banmali, Us Path Par Tum Dena Phaink,
Matra Bhoomi Per Sheesh Chadhaney, Jis Path Jaayen Veer Anek.

Last time, when I was here in 2007, the memorial was still being developed. The memorial also has plaques for all the national heroes. There is an auditorium where you can watch a documentary on the Kargil War. Besides this , there is a canteen where you may enjoy tea and samosa. I presented a copy of my book 'Deshbhakti Ke Paawan Teerth' to the officer-in-charge on duty. After getting a briefing on the war, we set out for Kargil. Very soon, we reached Kaksar. The place reminded us of Captain Saurabh Kalia and Captain Amit Bhardwaj. They both were posted here. A bridge here has been named after Captain Amit Bhardwaj and a stadium after Captain Saurabh Kalia.

Captain Amit Bhardwaj

When Captain Saurabh Kalia and five other soldiers of 4 Jat Regiment, went missing from the Bajrang Post of Kaksar since 14th May 1999, Captain Amit Bhardwaj of the same regiment came forward to go in their search. Captain Saurabh Kalia and Captain Amit Bhardwaj were very close and had a special bonding—I was told about this by the mother of Captain Saurabh Kalia when I had gone to visit her at Palampur in Himachal Pradesh. Not only that, a photo of Captain Amit Bhardwaj is displayed with extreme regards in the memorial room of Captain Saurabh Kalia. On 17th May 1999, Captain

Amit Bhardwaj led a search party of 30 soldiers in a bid to find Captain Saurabh Kalia. They continued climbing snow-covered mountains for almost one and a half day and as they reached Bajrang Post, they noticed some different kind of activity there. He along with two soldiers was moving ahead when the enemy started firing on them indiscriminately. Captain Amit Bhardwaj got hit in his leg. Finding their leader injured, his men requested him to return to the base, but he was not ready to move. He kept confronting the enemy soldiers before he was hit in his belly. He made the supreme sacrifice for the country. His body laid on the mountains of Kaksar under enemy's captivity for almost two months before we retrieved it after Kaksar was recaptured by us. The biggest tragedy was that his parents could not even have the last glimpse of their son, as the body being too decomposed could not be taken out of the coffin. Even the last rites were performed along with the coffin. What could be more tragic than this for a parent?

I got an opportunity in 2020 to meet the family of Captain Amit Bhardwaj at Jaipur in Rajasthan. It gave a lot of satisfaction to touch the feet of his brave parents. Many points of Amit's life were discussed. Amit's elder sister Sunita Didi does her best to treasure his memories. She organises blood donation camp every year on Captain Amit's death anniversary. Children from many schools in Jaipur visit the memorial of Captain Amit Bhardwaj on the day to pay homage.

After these episodes of Captain Saurabh Kalia and Captain Amit Bhardwaj, it became quite clear that it was not the mujahideen who were involved in the infiltrations but Pakistani soldiers were; though Pakistan was constantly refuting this charge. The pressure was steadily building up on India to testify this fact.

I would like to mention here that the Kargil warzone was strategically divided into six main sectors:

1. Drās, 2. Mushkoh, 3. Kaksar, 4. Kargil, 5. Batalik 6. Turtuk.

On 11th May 1999, 1 Naga was the first to be called and asked to capture Tololing and some other peaks in Drās instantly. Three peaks—Tololing, Tiger Hill and Point 4875, were critical for us in the Kargil War, especially in Drās sub-sector, as the enemy was able to strike at our Highway with ease from these points. 8 Sikh regiment of the Indian Army joined the operation at Drās on 15th May.

Even on 19th May 1999, GOC of 15th Corps i.e., General Officer Commanding Lt Gen Krishna Pal, who was responsible for the security of this region, was still terming this incident as a case of local infiltration.

However, the deteriorating situation was constantly pointing to some major incursion. But they were at a loss to take any major action in the absence of some credible information. Even Brigade Commander Brigadier Surender Singh did not have any justifiable information. When the

Commanding Officer of 1 Naga, before launching attack, requested information about the likely size of the enemy contingent over Tololing peak, he was given a figure of around 20. But, at that point of time, our intelligence agencies could not apprehend the exact number of intruders. It was not only the government intelligence but even the military intelligence had been unsuccessful. It is not that firing had started only in the May of 1999. There had been innumerable instances of firing by Pakistan soldiers on the LOC in the last few years. But they were just being ignored terming them as minor incidents. Besides this, it was also clear by now that even our surveillance had deficiencies. As it is, some bits of information were available with every intelligence agency including RAW (Research & Analysis Wing), IB (Intelligence Bureau), Army Intelligence and state intelligence, but none of the agencies could decipher the main signal by linking together those bits and pieces. The Kargil Review Committee that went through complete analysis of the war, had identified 45 such vital inputs; this number was later pruned to 11 by the National Security Council and Joint Intelligence Committee. This also makes it evident that various security and intelligence agencies did lack coordination.

On the plains, The then Minister of Defence, George Fernandes was doing all out efforts to lift the morale of the Army. But, perhaps due to some confusion, he announced that the infiltrators would be driven off our land within the next 48 hours. As I have mentioned earlier, Northern Army Commander Lt Gen Hari Mohan Krishna was on leave. There was however some solace when the Chief of Army returned from his foreign tour on 20th May. He reviewed the situation on return and immediately got in touch with the Chief of Air Staff and the Chief of Naval Staff to finalise the strategy for the next move. By then, the Army had already announced its Operation Vijay' campaign to remove Pakistan infiltrators from our land.

General V. P. Malik was in favour of using Air Force to drive off enemy sitting at the peaks. The Air Chief placed the proposal on the government's table. In the initial period, CCS i.e., Cabinet Committee on Security had some of its own preconceptions, but very soon, the Air Force launched its own 'Operation White Ocean.' On 21st May, the Air Force deployed its aircraft Canberra for a reconnaissance mission in the Batalik region. Squadron Leader Jha and Group Captain Perumal were flying the same. Within 90 minutes of its take off from Agra base, the aircraft was flying over the Batalik region. Jha immediately started capturing pictures of the Line of Control area. He asked Perumal to bring the aircraft down a little to enable him to capture clear pictures. Suddenly they experienced a strong jolt and soon realised that the aircraft had been hit by an anti-aircraft missile by the enemy. Perumal somehow composed himself and managed to land safely at the Srinagar air base. Both the government and the Army were stunned to see the pictures brought by them; they clearly revealed the extent of incursions and the level of preparedness of the enemy. The

Indian Air Force launched air strikes formally on 26th May 1999. However, high altitudes and harsh weather conditions limited the impact of these air strikes, rather they even resulted in some losses that we may never forget.

On 27th May 1999, Squadron Ldr Ajay Ahuja and Flt Lt Nachiketa were sent on MIG 21 and MIG 27 to take pictures of Kargil peaks in order to correctly spot the enemy locations. Suddenly, Nachiketa's aircraft caught fire and he reported on radio that he was jumping out of the aircraft. He jumped out but his plane crashed in the Batalik mountains. As a senior, Squadron Ldr Ajay Ahuja got worried about Nachiketa's safety.

He lowered his plane and got hit by enemy's Stinger Missile. Pakistan soldiers captured Nachiketa. His life was saved. However, Ajay Ahuja was not fortunate enough. He did jump out of his burning plane but got caught by the enemy. He was later tortured and brutally killed by them. This was a heinous crime and was widely protested. Pakistan became the target of public anger. A huge protest was staged outside the Pakistan Embassy in New Delhi. Not only public, even the Army was shocked by the killing of Sqn Ldr Ajay Ahuja. The entire country was in a state of mourning.

Squadron Ldr Ajay Ahuja

I got an opportunity to meet Smt. Alka Ahuja, wife of the hero Ajay Ahuja, on the 20th anniversary of the Kargil War. She manages a petrol pump allotted in the name of Ajay Ahuja in Okhla area of South Delhi. I requested her to share some memories related to Ajay Ahuja. She did oblige. I quote below her words,

> That was a day in the month of May 1999 when Ajay and I were alone at home in Bhatinda and we were just chatting. He said, "Dear, we did not even notice it is already 10 years since our marriage." I felt happy to hear that. That was because it really gave me satisfaction to know that he was happy with his married life. On the 15th of the same month, i.e., 15 May 1999, a party was organised for all officers in the Air Force mess. Everybody was talking about Srinagar in that party. Ajay had been posted at some other air base at that time. Ajay had gone to Srinagar on duty just a few days back, still I did enquire with his colleagues present there whether Ajay also was to go there (Srinagar) again. They said, "No."
>
> On Monday, 17th May 1999, he (Ajay) took charge as Flight Commander of the squadron. I received a call from Ajay the same day. He said that he was going to Srinagar. He also asked me to prepare his bag and send the same to the squadron. Ajay's birthday falls on 22nd May and hence, I assumed he would be back by the 22nd. Accordingly, I also kept one set of his dress ready for his birthday party. I received his call on the

22nd . I wished him for his birthday and asked about his return. But he said he was required at Srinagar for some more time and hence, Ankur (our son) and I could travel to Srinagar to join him. He asked me to remit some money to enable him to arrange for our flight tickets.

Ankur was really excited and was jumping with joy all around the house, as he was to see his 'Dayda' (he affectionately called his father as 'Dayda') very soon. But it was our misfortune that all the flights to Srinagar were cancelled. We were not aware of the reason for the cancellation. We were also not able to contact Ajay.

We had no idea at all that there was tension at the border. Only after air strikes started on 26th May, we came to know about that. On 27th May, I felt some uneasiness coupled with headache. The same day, the Station Commander in his official uniform, came to our house along with one of my friends. Usually when an officer comes to your house in uniform, it signals seriousness of the situation.

I was surprised to see the officer and I abruptly asked my friend why he was there? The officer accompanying my friend informed me, "Ahuja has got separated from his group and is missing since then." I felt heart-broken, as it was evening and Ajay was in a mountainous region. There was no news about him. He had lost contact with his group around 11:30 am.

I was just praying to God, but I received a message at 8 o'clock that Ajay was no more!

I came to know later that Flt Lt Nachiketa had lost contact with his group and Ajay had spotted his location. Ajay only was directing the helicopter pilot to that location. In the meanwhile,

Ajay's plane was hit by enemy missile as the enemy was positioned right inside our LOC area. Even after that, Ajay had safely ejected from the damaged plane. But unfortunately, the enemy soldiers caught him and took him under custody. He was tortured and later brutally killed by the ruthless enemy.

As our 5-year-old son was too excited to meet his Dayda, I just could not gather courage to tell him that he would not be able to see his 'Dayda' any more. Ajay did return home, but wrapped in tricolour. We could not see him for the last time. The little kid performed the last rites of his father, without knowing what actually he was doing.

I could not tell him anything about his father. But one day, he asked me, "Mummy, now Dayda will not return ever, isn't it?" His words still echo in my ears. And then, the 5-year-old little kid suddenly turned into a matured person. After that day, he stopped talking about his father lest he upset his mother. He never wept for his father. All these things did influence him severely.

Then, I had to get stronger, as my son also was in pain. I did not know what I should do next, as we were living a nomadic life. We were just shifting from one place to another. I moved to Delhi and took up a job in Air Force School as a teacher, as I was otherwise also teaching independently. Then BJP government had announced allotment of petrol pumps to family members of servicemen.

My father had completed all formalities for the same. However, I was a bit reluctant, as none in my family had till then taken up business as a profession and I was assuming that to be really difficult. In the meantime, Punjab Government offered me a PCS job and I moved to Chandigarh. My parents stayed with us because of my son, but I lost my father the same year in December. I was then feeling as if I was back to square one. Just next day after the death of my father, I received a letter from HPCL regarding allotment of petrol pump.

That was really a difficult time, as I had lost even my father who was my greatest inspiration and well-wisher at that time. I had to resign from my job at Chandigarh, as it was difficult to manage the same with a little kid. I returned to Delhi and started working for the petrol pump, as I wanted to settle in life for my son and I had family support at Delhi. The life is completely changed now. We could not even see Ajay at that time, but that has given me strength to face the challenges of life. I feel Ajay would someday return with his smiling face, as he wanted to make his wife a strong person. The wait continues.

— Alka Ahuja

On the very next day after that incident of 27th May 1999 i.e., on 28th May, Pakistan shot down our MI helicopter killing five of our soldiers. It was felt then, that the decision for the use of the Air Force was somehow not fruitful. But, the morale of our Air Force was quite high and they inducted Mirage 2000 in the war. It did work like a miracle and we started to see some favourable results. The success of the Air Force inspired the Army also. The feat achieved by the Air Force in the Batalik sector was beyond expectation. The Air Force wiped out the Pakistani base camp at Muntho Dhalo. As per some estimates, some 160 Pakistani soldiers were killed in the fierce attack by the Indian Air Force. This severely dented Pakistan's morale.

There, the Indian Army could lay hands on identity cards on the bodies of some soldiers, proving that they were regular Pakistani soldiers. India was waiting for this very evidence, as Pakistan was constantly maintaining that mujahideen and not the Pakistani soldiers were involved in the infiltrations. We gradually collected many such evidences and proved on several international platforms that the Pakistan Army was directly involved in the same.

The 1 Naga and Garhwal Rifles was assigned the task of capturing Point 5140. They however could not be successful in their attempt. There were many reasons for the same like fury of the weather, wrong assessment and lack of snow boots and inadequate winter clothes. At the same time, lack of information about exact location of the enemy was also a major reason. The mission of capturing the 16000-ft high Tololing peak was assigned to the 18 Grenadiers that was then posted in Ganderbal area of Kashmir. On 15th May 1999, they were ordered to immediately move to Drās. On 18th May, the 18 Grenadiers reported at 121st Mountain Brigade Headquarters at Matayan.

Before the war, the task of security of the entire Drās region was assigned to the 16 Grenadiers; but they had failed in their task. However, we cannot blame a single regiment for such a widespread infiltration; in fact, all the security agencies of the country, local intelligence agencies and military intelligence agencies were responsible for the same. There are evidences that suggest that Pakistan initially planned to capture few posts in Drās region only, but when they arrived and found large stretches of plains vacant there, they went on extending their hold and finally stopped with their control over 160 posts along the 150-kilometres long Line of Control. It is not that we did not get any hint of the same; we did have some information about infiltrations but never took the same with seriousness and treated them only as limited infiltrations that occur occasionally in the region. Nobody had ever imagined that so much would happen at such a large scale.

This part of the Line of Control is quite complex. The geographical attributes of the region are extremely arduous. There are high mountain ranges that are the sources of Himalayan rivers. The passes and heavy snowfalls create horrendous conditions in the region making it impossible to stay there. As per some estimates, regular patrolling was not being carried out for around 80-kilometres long stretch of the Line of Control because of these geographical impediments. More or less, this arrangement was going on for the last 52 years. Who would have known that the neighbour was harbouring some evil intentions?

Commanding Officer Colonel Khushal Singh Thakur of the 18 Grenadiers accepted this challenge and promptly got into planning for the victory over Tololing. Without wasting a moment, Col Thakur set out for a recce of Tololing on 20th May. He took all the points into account that were vital for the victory. He planned for three-pronged assault on Tololing. Major Rajesh Singh Adhikari of the 18 Grenadiers was craving for victory, as a victory over Tololing would have worked as a morale booster for the Army soldiers. On 26th May, Maj Adhikari even flew on a helicopter, identified the enemy bunkers and fired on them, but the helicopter could not achieve much success due to inclement weather.

Major Rajesh Singh Adhikari

The month of May was coming to an end and the victory still appeared to be remote. The enemy was firing on us as easy targets, that also at their own will and convenience. We were helpless and though ready, were unable to do anything. Ultimately, there came some good news on 29th May when Maj Rajesh Singh Adhikari succeeded in securing the Hump near Tololing. However, he could not hold on to the same for long. Maj Adhikari laid down his life. I would like to mention here that the Hump area is divided into ten sectors. As per their devious plan, the enemy knowingly kept the body of Maj Rajesh Singh Adhikari enmeshed in cross firing. Our pain increased further when we failed to recover his body from there for many days.

Lt Col Vishwanathan

On 2nd June 1999, Second-in-Command Lt Col Vishwanathan was deployed for the Tololing mission. Pressure from higher authorities was building up many-fold because of constant failures. A significant reason for the failure here also was the fact that the Army had not received expected artillery support till that time. You would know later how Artillery discharged its crucial duty in creating history during the Kargil War. Particularly, deployment of Bofors guns completely changed the course of the war.

Lt Col Vishwanathan also tried his best but could not get desired results. He would have definitely succeeded had he received 'Artillery' support on time; but this did not happen and he lost his life. But before laying down his life, he had bravely challenged the enemy. Along with him, Subedar Randhir Singh had also demonstrated extraordinary valour and laid down his life. Both these heroes were awarded 'Veer Chakra' posthumously.

A little before being martyred, Lt Col Vishwanathan had written a letter to his father. In that emotional letter, he had asked his father to take care of his family. He probably had realised that it was not possible for him to return alive from the mission he was going to lead.

Commanding Officer Col Khushal Thakur was badly shattered by the martyrdom of his Second-in-Command. It appeared to be his personal loss. All the higher officials were shocked by the sacrifice of Lt Col Vishwanathan. By now, it had become crystal clear that it was impossible to get a grip over the enemy without the support of heavy artillery and firepower. The pressure to secure victory over the enemy was just building up. But the situation on the ground was quite disappointing. The Army was still unaware of the number and locations of the enemy.

For the entire month of May, we kept on recovering bodies of our soldiers from the high mountains. The success that was required to gain the upper hand in the war was eluding us. There was deep sense of gloom all around. There was only one thing that was in our favour, and that was our soldiers' morale that was impossible to shake. Our primary aim was to drive off the enemy from our land under any circumstances, even if that required the sacrifice of our soldiers. General V. P. Singh announced that we would continue our fight on the strength of available resources only. His statement was enough to boost the morale of our soldiers. This is where Pakistan made a miscalculation. As I have mentioned earlier, Musharraf and his pawns were assuming that India would never be able to launch direct assault because of geographical complexities. But India broke their illusion.

Till then, three assaults had been launched on Tololing but all with insignificant success. But yes, the 18 Grenadiers had created ground for subsequent attacks and learnt some significant lessons that they shared with other regiments. These experiences came in handy for our victory later.

On 29th May, Maj Sarvanan of the 1 Bihar Regiment demonstrated unprecedented valour in the Batalik sector. He was assigned the task of capturing the Zubar Top. Conquering the mountains of 14000-ft high Zubar Complex was quite difficult, especially when you do not have artillery support. The 1 Bihar had only recently arrived from Assam and it immediately set out on its mission. Maj Sarvanan succeeded in demolishing six security barriers laid by the enemy. Even his own men were also amazed to watch his indomitable ability, spirit

Maj Sarvanan

and courage. He went on moving forward and challenging the enemy. The only son of his mother and only brother of his sister, he had once said that he had two mothers—*one his own mother and the other Mother India, and he would serve Mother India before serving his own mother*. He was making his statement true that day. But luck was not on our side. It played the same game with Maj Sarvanan that it had played with Maj Rajesh Singh Adhikari on Tololing. He laid down his life, but we could not recover his body for 45 days as we gained victory over Zubar Top only after 45 days. Maj Sarvanan was posthumously honoured with 'Veer Chakra' for this extraordinary act of valour.

On 7th June 1999, Brigadier Lakhwinder Singh of Artillery deployed Bofors guns in the entire Drās sector. These very guns later proved to be game-changer. The enemy cried in pain wherever Bofors fired. We were now fully ready for big strikes. For us, Tololing was the first major target. Not only millions of Indians but also the Rajputana Rifles and the 18 Grenadiers were eagerly waiting to fly the tricolour over Tololing. The night of 11th June was decided for the assault and everybody was pumped up because of the artillery support being made available. This was the first major assault when we were looking mentally, physically and strategically strong. The Commanding Officer did not want to take any chances. 11th June was a Friday and many of our soldiers believed that it would be difficult to defeat Pakistan on a Friday.

Although, this was just a notion, the assault was postponed to 12th June keeping the feelings of the soldiers in mind. Meanwhile, an interesting incident occurred. The India-Pakistan match of the Cricket World Cup in England was scheduled for 8th June. All the commanders were praying for India's victory, as this would have further boosted the morale of our soldiers. Anyway, that is what happened, India won the match by 47 runs. Rahul Dravid scored a maximum of 61 runs. The Indian camp was in high spirits.

Meanwhile, a piece of news aroused the fire of anger all around India on 9th June. Pakistan handed over the mutilated bodies of Captain Saurabh Kalia and other soldiers, who had gone towards the Line of Control on 15th May to assess the situation, to India. The condition of the bodies proved that before being killed, they were brutally tortured, the ill-treatment meted out them is a blot on humanity and that was the meanest kind that may be difficult to even imagine. There was a wave of anger across the country on hearing this. There was no doubt that all this was a plot of the Pakistan Army only. In the war history of India, this was the most brutal, heinous and disgusting act that enraged the entire country. The sacrifice of Captain Saurabh Kalia and his fellow soldiers infused new life into the Kargil War and secured a victory in this war became the solitary aim of our soldiers.

❑

4

Beginning of the Victory

The Rajputana Rifles were then posted at Kupwara in Kashmir. On 25th May, they received an order to proceed to Drās immediately. Then on 29th May, the regiment reported at Matayan. The mission to attack Tololing was immediately assigned. Fortunately, Raj Rif (Rajputana Rifles) got some time to prepare and also, soldiers got some time to acclimatize themselves. In the meantime, they also arranged snow boots, sleeping bags, down jackets and some other materials that were helpful in fighting at a height of 16000 ft. They were preparing themselves both physically and mentally, to fight at that height. Raj Rif Commanding Officer Lt Col Ravindra Nath had a huge responsibility to discharge. He had to come up to the expectations of the people of his country. He got the opportunity to add to the saga of Kargil's victory to the golden history of the Rajputana

Lt Col Ravindra Nath

Rifles; he did not want to lose the same at any cost. Tololing is not just a peak; it is actually a complex having few other peaks also namely Tololing (Point 4590), Tololing Top, Barbaad Bunker, Hump, Three Pimples, Naul and Lone. All the details, including the minutest ones, relating to all the above segments were collected and discussed with colleagues to develop a comprehensive plan. A victory over Tololing would have proved that the enemy was not invincible and that the Indian Army was capable of dealing with any possible attack. Secondly, it was essential to send a positive and confident message from the Army to their countrymen and the most important job was to secure a large segment of our National Highway. The Raj Rif utilised every moment of the 10-12 days it had, to prepare for the mission. It was now time for the Raj Rif to show the capability it is known for.

Finally, the day of 12th June that everybody was waiting for, arrived The 18 Grenadiers were told to relax. The experiences of the 18 Grenadiers were quite useful for developing the plan for the attack. For the Raj Rif, it was like a golden moment. They had to prove themselves that day. Raj Rif Commanding Officer Lt Col Ravindra Nath made an emotional address to his soldiers. He said, "My dear sons, I just want Tololing, somehow or other." On hearing

Subedar Bhanwar Lal

this, Subedar Bhanwar Lal said, "Saheb, you will have your morning tea at Tololing." That response from Subedar Bhanwar Lal, brimming with self-confidence, and his absolute faith in his Commanding Officer lifted all the soldiers' spirits greatly. It was going to be a do-or-die battle. Everybody chanted 'Raja Ramchandra Ki Jai'.

At 6:30 pm, 120 guns collected from all across Drās were deployed on the National Highway facing Tololing and firing began. It looked like Drās was having a massive firecracker show. Those 120 guns included many Bofors guns also. Along with the guns, many Russian-made MBRLs (Multi Barrel Rocket Launchers) were also spewing fire. All of them continued to rain fire on Tololing Hill for six hours consecutively and created mayhem in the enemy's camp.

The Artillery was providing all logistics support to the infantry that day which was crucial for a victory. The officers and soldiers climbing up the hill were directing the guns, based on their own estimates, to aim at the enemies' locations. That was possible as they had radio sets to talk to the Artillery Officer on the ground. For the first time, it appeared the day was going to be fruitful. The artillery support was making the soldiers feel very emotionally strong. The 8 Mountain Division, which was in charge of this region, was also watching the action closely. The Raj Rif had made large-scale preparations for this battle.

But Brigadier Lakhwinder Singh was facing a peculiar problem. In fact, Pakistan had WLR i.e.,

'Weapon Locating Radar' procured from the United States of America; this equipment was capable to detect and locate enemies Artillery locations. In that case, the enemy could return fire at our guns. The only remedy was to reposition our guns a bit left or right immediately after firing. Fortunately, this 'Jugad' formula worked. As such, our Army had been making attempts for years to acquire the Weapon Locating Radar, but for some reasons, that did not materialise. However, it is pleasing to note that, as of today, the Army is equipped with all such state-of-the-art weapons.

In the meanwhile, the enemy's message was heard on the wireless system, "Janaab, all hell has broken loose here!". Tololing was that day being pounded from three sides.

The enemy sitting on height is always in an advantageous position. But it appeared that with the help of the Artillery, we could succeed in hoisting our tricolour on Tololing peak that very day. The war was at its peak. It was past midnight. Frozen ice at many places at Tololing had made it quite slippery. Maj Vivek Gupta, hailing from Dehradun, had inherited the passion of patriotism from his father, retired Lt Col B R S Gupta. Braving all the odds, Maj Vivek Gupta led from the front and laid down his life for the pride of his motherland. He was posthumously honoured with 'Maha Vir Chakra'. You may call it his fate that, he got martyred on 13th June and it was the same 13th June in the year 1992 when he had joined the Rajputana Rifles. Next day, when his body was flown to Delhi, his wife

Captain (Dr.) Rajshree Gupta

Captain (Dr) Rajshree Gupta, who is also an officer in the Army Medical Corps, was there in uniform to pay her last respect to him. As a wife to salute the body of her husband at an emotional moment like this— it demonstrated her dutifulness, thinking, determination and courage. I would never be able to forget her photo that had appeared in 'India Today' at that time.

Another brave heart, Naik Digendra Singh demonstrated extreme valour in the war and single-handedly shot down 48 Pakistanis. He and his team were assigned the task of demolishing the first and the last of 11 bunkers built over Tololing. They executed the job quite efficiently. It is said that after hoisting the victory flag, Naik Digendra Singh had beheaded a Pakistani captain and carried his head with him on his way back; this was a matter of discussion in Drās for many days. Soldiers from far off places would come to have look at the head. The severed head was making a positive emotional impact on the soldiers. The head was buried after some time. Naik Digendra Singh was honoured with 'Maha Vir Chakra' for his demonstration of extraordinary valour. Other brave hearts of the Rajputana Rifles like Havildar Sultan Singh, Company Havildar Major Yashvir Singh and Lance Naik Bachan Singh wrote a new saga of heroism in the regiment's history and imprinted their names forever in the war history of India.

Captain Vijyant Thapar, having the nickname 'Robin', was assigned the mission of capturing the 'Barbaad Bunker' on Tololing. He found a unique way of firing up his soldiers. While going for the assault, he played the famous song 'Sandese aate hain...' of the film 'Border' on his Walkman. And then launched an attack on the enemy with full force and dynamism. Demonstrating his valour and bravery, Robin shot down two Pakistani infiltrators and completed his mission. Robin called his mother from the war zone using satellite phone and conveyed the news of his victory. Who would have thought that this youth of 22 years was soon going to lay down his life for the country?

Capt. Vijyant Thapar

The words of Subedar Bhanwar Lal ultimately proved to be true. The news that everybody was very impatiently waiting for was conveyed over wireless at 4 am of 13th June 1999. It was the news of victory over Tololing. Lt Col Ravindra Nath first of all conveyed the news to his senior officers and started climbing up the Tololing. After all, he had to have tea there! Unfortunately, Subedar Bhanwar Lal was not there to see all this. He had laid down his life. Lt Col Ravindra Nath did reach the top of Tololing, but he was quite distressed, as he had lost 10 of his soldiers and another 25 were injured. Havildar Sultan Singh, Company Havildar Maj Yashvir Singh and Subedar Bhanwar Lal were posthumously honoured with 'Vir Chakra'. Lt Col Ravindra Nath was awarded 'Vir Chakra' and promoted as Colonel. This victory of 13th June generated a wave of joy across the country. The people of India have always shown love and respect for the army and reposed trust in them. Children and common people started writing letters in thousands of numbers to their heroes in the war zones to cheer them up.

One thing that had become clear by now was the fact that the bunkers (Bunker have been referred to as 'Sangar' in the Kargil War) that Pakistan had built were well fortified. Iron sheets had been used in their construction. After getting covered with heavy boulders, they provided security like a fort. An idea of their strength can be gauged by the fact that they were able to easily withstand even the attacks of rocket launchers. The fortification was blatantly revealing how leisurely they had been built. They made us believe that the Pakistani soldiers had already infiltrated by December 1998 or January 1999.

The Tololing victory had relieved the Indian Army from acute mental pressure. Pakistan, who had been assuming that they were invincible because of their higher positions, had been proved wrong. Sources reveal that Pakistan took three days to officially acknowledge India's victory over Tololing. The people in power there, were not ready to believe that. There is no doubt that this long-awaited victory did take its toll—we had to lose a number of our soldiers. The then Prime Minister Atal Bihari Vajpayee paid a visit to Kargil on 13th June to cheer up our soldiers and assured the Army of all possible help. The Tololing victory of 13th June had already boosted the morale of the Indian Army. Same day, the Air Force launched a major offensive attack in the Batalik sector.

Pakistan's Foreign Minister Sartaj Aziz visited New Delhi on 12th June; however, a major exposure had already taken place by then. On 11th June, our then Minister of Foreign Affairs had made the conversation between Pakistan Army Chief Pervez Musharraf and his Commander, public and that too in the presence of media. This conversation had taken place on 26th May and 29th May when Musharraf was on an official visit to China. It is believed that the recording of this conversation was managed by the intelligence agencies of India. This recording proved to be quite valuable for India. On one hand, Pakistan was fooling the world by claiming that only mujahideen were involved in infiltrations into

India, while on the other hand, this recording proved that this was the handiwork of the Pakistan Army. Pakistan had been completely exposed. Pakistan's evil plan was now crystal clear in front of the world. Our then foreign minister Jaswant Singh expressed his displeasure by not shaking hands with Aziz. Dejected Aziz returned to Pakistan.

The Tololing victory caused a dent in the Pakistan camp. Pakistan realised that the Kargil War was a major mistake on its part. Over and above that, there was pressure from even the United States of America for a ceasefire. The international community welcomed India's decision not to cross the Line of Control. In the same course, the then American President, Bill Clinton told Nawaz Sharif in clear terms to withdraw his forces from Indian territory as soon as possible; and he also appreciated India for exercising restraint. In order to muster support at the international level, our National Security Advisor (NSA) Brajesh Mishra reached Geneva to meet G-8 leaders and explained India's position on the war; he also handed over a letter to Bill Clinton from PM Vajpayee that conveyed that India was losing its patience swiftly. The United States assured a solution within a few days.

❑

5

Ye Dil Mange More

After Tololing, our next target was to hoist our tricolour over Point 5140. The mission to attain this target was assigned to the 13th Battalion of the Jammu & Kashmir Rifles Regiment, led by Lt Col Yogesh Kumar Joshi. Last year he had been superannuated as Lt Gen and Army Commander of Northern Command. The 13 JAK Rif (J&K Rifles) reported to 56 Mountain Brigade on 8th June, 1999. They were immediately conveyed details of their mission. Lt Col Joshi, with all his passion and devotion, started to prepare for the victory. Along with JAK Rif, 18 Garhwal and 1 Naga were also deployed for this mission.

Lt Col Yogesh Kumar Joshi

The time of assault was scheduled at 9:30 pm on 19th June. 'C' and 'D' companies were positioned for the same—'C' i.e., the Charlie Company that was led by 24-year-old Captain Vikram Batra and 'D' i.e., the Delta Company that was being commanded by 25-year-old Captain Sanjeev Jamwal. Each company had 120 soldiers. At 9:30 pm, both the companies marched towards Point 5140 chanting 'Durga Mata Ki Jai'. Captain Sanjeev Jamwal and Captain Vikram Batra invited their Commanding Officer for the morning tea at Point 5140. The Artillery guns had started spewing fire right at 9:30 pm. The platoon brimming with excitement marched ahead in that chilling cold at a height of 16000 ft. There were a total of 7 sangars of the enemy at Point 5140; they all were to be demolished that day before hoisting the victory flag.

Captain Vikram Batra

The infantry used to get the cover fire of the Artillery but stopped on reaching some 200 to 400 metres away from the enemy; that was to ensure that our own soldiers did not become, victims of that firing. When Captain Vikram Batra and Captain Sanjeev Jamwal were just 200 metres away from the enemy sangars, they also asked the Artillery to stop firing. But, when they later realised that the enemy was still beyond their reach, they courageously decided to take a unique risk. They asked the Artillery to continue firing until they reached within 100 metres of those sangars. The Commanding Officer Lt Col Y K Joshi, sitting below was a bit worried on this decision. This could be quite dangerous. In such a case, our soldiers could have been victims of our own firing. However, the officer leading in the war zone is the best person to assess the situation there. The Artillery provided the required support to Vikram and Sanjeev. This helped both the companies to reach very close to the enemy bunkers and launch a fierce assault.

One by one, all the seven sangars were attacked with hand grenades and subsequently captured.

Captain Vikram Batra checked his watch; it was 3:25 in the morning. First of all, Captain Sanjeev Jamwal uttered his code over radio set, "Oh Ya Ya." Captain Vikram Batra also immediately squealed with joy, "Ye Dil Mange More." These were their victory codes. On getting this message, Lt Col Joshi promptly started climbing up towards the peak. He had to have his tea there! The news that not a single life had been lost in the entire operation brought tears in his eyes. He later mentioned that the entire operation was meticulously executed. God and luck were with us and all the people in our team had given their best. The 13 JAK Rif proved that no enemy could stand against their courage, bravery and heroism.

For this victory, Lt Col Joshi, Captain Sanjeev Jamwal, Naik Dev Prakash and Rifleman Mehar Singh were awarded 'Vir Chakra' and Havildar Mohan Lal, Rifleman Ajay Pathania, Rifleman Sunil Kumar and Rifleman Kewal Kumar were honoured with 'Sena Medal'. The name of Captain Vikram Batra was recommended for the 'Maha Vir Chakra'.

But, he was destined for 'Param Vir Chakra' that was awarded to him later, though posthumously, after the victory over Point 4875. On 20th June, the photo of the entire team along with arms and ammunition recovered from the enemy and the tricolour flying on the peak went viral across the entire country. With the victory over Point 5140, the entire Tololing sector had come under our control and this was the turning point for the victory in this war.

The victory of the Army over Point 5140 made Captain Vikram Batra the cynosure of all eyes across the country. He looked no less than a rock star on television. He only coined the new war cry 'Ye Dil Mange More'. People across the country were ready to make any sacrifice for the country. The passion of patriotism and the eagerness to drive off the enemy from the peaks in Kargil were clearly visible in the eyes of Captain Vikram Batra. The enemy also acknowledged his bravery and his code name 'Shershah' became famous in the enemy camp also. In our country, people coined quite a few titles like 'Kargil Hero', 'Lion of Drās' and 'Tiger of Drās' for him. On 20th June, Vikram talked to his parents over satellite phone and told them about his victory. His mother blessed him and asked him never to look back while discharging his duty. Vikram did follow his mother's words. The name of Vikram Batra created a sense of fear even in the Pakistan camp.

The media across the country was giving this latest hero of the youth an excellent coverage. Who

Author at Srinagar Railway Station

Major Somnath Sharma's memorial built in front of Srinagar Airport

Author at the banks of Dal Lake

Entrance Gate of Mata Kheer Bhawani Temple

Idol of Mata Kheer Bhawani

Beautiful view of Matayen

This milestone on 43 Complex thrills you

View of Pakistan's border area from 43 Complex

Bird's Eye View of Zoji La Pass

Beautiful view of the Himalayas from the author's car passing through Zoji La Pass

View of road leading from Kargil to LOC

Author at Zoji La Pass

Bird's eye view of the Shingo River near the Kargil-LOC road

Bird's eye view of Tiger Hill

This board warns while entering Kargil

Bird's eye view of the Himalayas near Baltal

Bird's eye view of the Himalayas near Baltal

A place called Pandaras near Dras

Author at Dras, in the background you can see Tiger Hill

This board itself is creating excitement

Author outside the Kargil War Memorial

An interior view of the Kargil War Memorial

The Kargil War Memorial

Seized Pakistani bunker displayed inside the Kargil War Memorial

Seized weapons from Pakistan on display at the Kargil War Memorial

Confiscated Pakistani Flag on display at the Kargil War Memorial

Kargil War Memorial

Author inside the Kargil War Memorial, in front of the name plaques of the soldiers who died during the Kargil War

Author with his friends inside the Kargil War Memorial

Author presenting his book to an army officer at the Kargil War Memorial

Author presenting his book to Ms Charulatha, wife of Major P Acharya, MVC

Author with this friends at Sando Top

Martyr Captain Saurabh Kalia of 4th Jat Regiment along with his five other comrades Arjun Ram Baswana, Bhanwar Lal Bagaria, Bhikha Ram Moondh, Mula Ram and Naresh Singh

Author presenting his book to Ms Meena Nayyar, mother of Captain Anuj Nayyar, MVC

Temple built in honour of martyrs in Mushkoh Valley

Captain Majoj Kumar Pandey's statue installed at his house

The road leading to Captain Majoj Kumar Pandey's Lucknow residence

Author offering homage to Captain Vijayant Thapar, VC at his home in Noida, Uttar Pradesh

MiG-21 fighter aircraft displayed at the Kargil War Memorial

Captain Vikram Batra

'Param Vir Chakra', the highest gallantry award conferred to Captain Vikram Batra

Memorial built at Captain Saurabh Kalia's Palampur residence

Author presenting his book to Ms Nutan Batra Malik, sister of Captain Vikram Batra, PVC

Author at at Captain Saurabh Kalia's house with Captain's mother Mrs. Vijay Kalia, father Dr. N.K. Kalia and brother Mr. Vaibhav Kalia

Childhood photograph of Captain Saurabh Kalia with his mother Mrs. Vijay Kalia, father Dr. N.K. Kalia and brother Mr. Vaibhav Kalia

'Tololing Peak' is seen in the background at the Kargil War Memorial

Memorial built in memory of Captain Kenguruse at Nerhema, Kohima

Author with Mrs. Bhanwari Devi, wife of Martyr Bhikha Ram Moondh of 4th Jat Regiment

Author with Colonel Balwan Singh

Author at Captain Amit Bhardwaj's house with Captain's mother Mrs. Sushila Sharma and father Mr. O.P. Sharma

Author at Captain Manoj Kumar Pandey's house with Captain's mother Mrs. Mohini Pandey and younger brother Mr. Manmohan Pandey

Author at Captain Vikram Batra's house with Captain's mother Mrs. Kamal Kant Batra and father Mr. Girdhari Lal Batra

Captain Vikram Batra during the Kargil War

The author with the three living 'Param Vir Chakra' winners Subedar Sanjay Kumar, Captain Yogendra Singh yadav and Captain Bana Singh (from left to right)

Panoramic view of Mushkoh Valley

Author paying homage to Captain Kenguruse in Nerhema, Kohima

Author presenting his book to the honorary Captain Yogendra Singh Yadav

Author with Colonel V.N. Thapar, father of Captain Vijyant Thapar, Veer Chakra

Author with Mrs. Alka Ahuja, wife of Squadron Leader Ajay Ahuja, Veer Chakra

Seeing this board in Dras, shivers run through one's body. In the background, you can see Tiger Hill

The board on the National Highway in Kargil which warn us that the enemy is watching us

Kargil View Gallery on Sando Top, opposite Tiger Hill

Author presenting his book to Subedar Major Sanjay Kumar, PVC

Panoramic view of Tiger Hill

Beautiful view of Mushkoh Valley

would have known that our 'Shershah' was very soon going to get confined to our hearts only!

This brave soldier of the JAK Rif Regiment, Captain Vikram Batra, was born on 9th September 1974 at Palampur in Himachal Pradesh. In April 2019, I got an opportunity to pay respect to the parents of this great son of the country. I also had the privilege of seeing the room where Vikram Batra lived. Now, the room is used to safely keep the items related to his life. His 'Param Vir Chakra' medal also graces that room, testifying the heroism that this brave heart had demonstrated in the battlefield while laying down his life for the country. His Army uniform also occupies a special place in the room. Neugal Café at Palampur was his favourite place. While talking to a friend there once, he had said, "*I will definitely come back, either after hoisting the tricolour or getting wrapped in the tricolour.*" His words have become a classic statement; even today, those words are inspiring the youth across the country.

While having tea at the Neugal Café, Palampur, I reminisced about Captain Vikram Batra. After visiting his house, I recollected one of his childhood memories. Back then, Doordarshan used to telecast a serial—'Param Vir Chakra'. It was produced by Chetan Anand and was based on the lives of the warriors who had been honoured with 'Param Vir Chakra'. This was Vikram's favourite show and he had been fascinated by the stories of war heroes. At that time, Batra family did not own a TV, due to which, Vikram went to his neighbours' place to watch that show. Thus, this show sowed the seed of patriotism and inculcated passion for the service uniform in Vikram Batra.

Major Sudhir Walia

Palampur is also considered to be the 'land of patriotic heroes' as this pious land is the birthplace of many great warriors. Prominent among them are—Major Somnath Sharma, Maj Sudhir Walia, Captain Vikram Batra and Captain Saurabh Kalia. Maj Somnath Sharma was even the first recipient of the 'Param Vir Chakra' which was awarded to him posthumously for the war against Pakistan during the years 1947-48. Before independence, a demonstration of extraordinary valour used to get honoured with the 'Victoria Cross'; which was replaced with 'Param Vir Chakra' post-independence.

Major Sudhir Walia also took part in the Kargil War; but a few months later, he laid down his life while fighting with terrorists in the Kashmir valley. He was honoured posthumously with 'Ashok Chakra'. 'Ashok Chakra' is the highest peacetime military decoration awarded for displaying extraordinary valour. Indeed there has to be something special in the land of Palampur!

❑

6

Chalte Chalte Mere Ye Geet Yaad Rakhna

If we believe the sources, Nawaz Sharif had understood by the middle of the month of June 1999 that he had fallen into the trap of Musharraf. By now, he had realised that Pakistan could not win Kargil war at any cost. The only feasible option was to somehow turn the tables of the war, keeping their throne safe. And for that, diplomacy had started behind-the-curtain. Pakistan was under tremendous international pressure, especially from the US government. On 23rd June, The United States deputed General Anthony Zinni to Islamabad to aggravate the pressure on the Pakistan government. Nawaz Sharif was running short of options. There were no takers for his lame argument that the Line of Control was not clearly depicted in the Shimla Agreement. Even China, the closest friend of Pakistan, did not support Pakistan; which led to a big diplomatic victory for India. India had realised by then that Nawaz Sharif had got caught in his own trap. Politically also, the Kargil War was nothing less than a litmus test for Atal Bihari Vajpayee. In India, Lok Sabha elections had already been announced. In these circumstances, any wrong step would lead to people's anger and Vajpayee would not prefer that. Atal Bihari Vajpayee was immensely hurt by the Kargil War, as he assessed that only a permanent arrangement with Pakistan could give way to peace, harmony and development in both the countries. The Kargil War had spoiled all his efforts. Now he did not want to take any chance further.

When we looked at the 'Three Pimples' peak from the Kargil War Memorial, I remembered that unfortunate night of 28th June 1999 when India lost the maximum number of soldiers, which also includes 3 officers. That instance of 28th June had wounded us badly. Its enormity can be gauged from the fact that a day post battle i.e. 29th June, the mess of the regiment remained closed.

On 28th June, 2 Rajputana Rifles and 18 Garhwal were again assigned a next to impossible mission—to capture Point 4700 and Black Rock area. Taking the plan for assault into perspective, 2 Rajputana Rifles segmented Black Rock area into various parts like Lone, Top, Bump, Tekri and Naul and made 'Kajal' their firebase. At a height of 16000 ft., there was a barren and unapproachable terrain with no place to hide and even the weather was severely cold. You could easily be targetted by the enemy there. Everybody knew that this was a do-or-die mission, with remote chance of survival. Who would

Major Padmapani Acharya

have known that the mission was going to be the toughest mission of the Indian Army till date and we were going to lose the maximum number of our soldiers. Major Padmapani Acharya, Captain Vijyant Thapar and Captain Kenguruse—all brave heroes entered the battlefield with an undying and resilient confidence. It was crucial to win the battle that day as that only would have allowed us to build a strong base there. The acquirement of this base was going to be valuable for securing victory further over Point 5100, which was essential to maintain our control over our National Highway.

Father of Maj Padmapani Acharya had served the Air Force as Wing Commander and had even participated in the wars against Pakistan in the years 1965 and in year 1971. Inspired by his father, Maj Padmapani Acharya was ready to lay down his life for the country. At that moment, he was remembering his wife Charulata who was pregnant. Vijyant and Acharya had lot of affection for each other. As a senior, Acharya took good care of Vijyant who in turn treated him as his idol. Before setting out for the battlefield, Major Acharya wrote a letter to his father and requested his father to read mythological stories to Charulata daily so that their to be born child would be cultured.

19 June, 1999
C/o 56 APO

Dear Papa,

Hope this letter finds you in the best of health and spirits. Thank you for your letter and card dated 14th June 1999.

We are also getting ready for our next task. Our unit has to live up to the higher expectations of the Army, Regiment as well as the media. You know what, even the Chief sent a letter of congratulations to the unit. It was indeed an honour for our unit to have been given such a task. Don't you think, hard work and sound ethos has its own merits? We now have to work harder to preserve the hopes and aspirations of our well-wishers.

Please do not worry about casualties. It is a professional hazard, which is beyond our control, so why worry; at least it is for a good cause. In the Bhagwad Gita, Lord Krishna briefs Arjun on the following lines: "*Hato va prapyasi swargam, Jitva va bhokshyase mahim, tasmaduttishtha kaunteya yuddhaya kritnishchayaha.*"

Prime Minister's Kargil visit was a good motivation. I am worth seeing, with an unkempt beard and Vaseline cream all over my ugly face to encounter the icy winds.

Please tell Maanam that combat is an honour of a lifetime and I would not think of anything less than that. What's a better way to serve the nation? I am proud to be in the Infantry and especially in our noted Battalion.

Take care of your health as well Maanam. Do not worry and lose sleep. Tell a Mahabharat story to Charu every day so that your grandchild imbibes good values.

Jai Mata Ki!

Yours affectionately
--Babloo
(P Acharya)

Capt. Vijyant Thapar

A little before this assault, Robin (nicknamed as Captain Vijyant Thapar) also had written a letter that was widely spread in the country. That letter revealed his feelings and ideology in front of all. In this letter, he had requested his father to continue sending Rs 50 to Rukhsana, a poor girl child from Kupwara' whose father was brutally killed by terrorists and she had gone into a coma out of fear. Robin's affection and encouragement had brought her out of that coma. Even now, Robin's father Col V N Thapar visits Rukhsana every year and their family continues to help her. Recently, Rukhsana cleared her 12th standard and as per her wish, Thapar family has gifted a laptop to her. Rukhsana also gifts a pack of apples every year to Col Thapar. This is going on uninterrupted for the last 17 years.

One line written by Robin in his last letter touched the heart of his father Col V N Thapar. Robin wrote, *"If you can, please come and see where the Indian Army fought for your tomorrow."* Col Thapar made these words as the aim of his life. Every year on the occasion of 'Kargil Vijay Diwas', he visits the hills of Naul where Robin had laid down his life. A small temple has been built there in his memory. At the age of 70 years, it is quite tough to visit Drās every year; there are no words to express the depth of Col Thapar's love for his son.

I am in regular touch with the Thapar family. In April 2020, when I met Col Thapar at his petrol pump in Noida, I was fortunate enough to spend around three hours with him. That day, he shared memories of Robin's life. I am sharing few lines written by him:

> 22 years have just flown by and the date of 28th June 2020 is just a few weeks away. We never missed Robin, as he never left us. Every morning, we remember him in our prayers, and our daily chats are never complete without a talk about Robin—had he been here, he would have laughed like this, he would have talked like that and he would have got annoyed like that. However, as the month of June approaches,

memories of Vijyant, the hills of Tololing and also the battle of Lone hill overwhelm our thoughts. That was one of the fiercest battles fought by the Indian Army. When we look back, we recollect that storm that came in Noida with the news of his sacrifice and shook all of us. That day, I was serving as a conveying authority in a court-martial at Alwar. Connectivity at Alwar was so poor that I was not getting any news. Hence, I could not even know when Robin along with his unit moved from Kupwara to Drās. Around 20th June, his mother told me over phone that 'India Today' had published the news relating to the operation of Robin and 2 Rajputana Rifles and I should get a copy of the magazine. But I could not lay my hands on the magazine at Alwar. Eventually, I received the news of his martyrdom over a phone call from Army Headquarters during my tea break. No idea why, but I could not believe the news. I just thought he might have got injured badly. When I left for Noida, I bought a copy of 'India Today' that had the news of the daring operation of the heroes of Tololing and 2 Rajputana Rifles. In the meanwhile, my wife also was informed about the loss of our son by the Army Headquarters. Later, their photographs and stories became the breaking news for all the TV channels and newspapers. The entire city appeared to be submerged in grief. While people from Meerut, Bulandshahr, Delhi and all across the country were arriving to our place to pay tribute, even VIPs and the underprivileged wanted to join in his last journey. Around 1.5 lakh people participated in his funeral. Passing through Drās and Srinagar, his body arrived at the base hospital in Delhi on 2nd July 1999. We have been told that on the night of the operation, Robin prioritized the evacuation of the injured to safe locations and then, with full determination, went on to launch the attack on the enemy. Robin had a fire and a flame of anger within that was exhorting him to settle scores on behalf of his friend, Saurabh Kalia and other martyrs. By that time, our soldiers had already secured a foothold on the hill.

However, he got deeply shocked when he received the news that his idol and favourite commander Major Padmapani Acharya had demised. That was the last bad news he received and then he surged ahead along with Naik Tilak Singh. The closest bunker of the enemy was just 15 metres away. There was indiscriminate firing from both ends. There was silence for some time and Robin took it as the best time to overpower the enemy. But fortune was not at his side! The moment he took his first step, he got hit in his head and we lost our beloved son. Fortunately, the Army and the country gained success in recapturing the hill.

Subsequently, a temple has been built at the place where Robin had attained martyrdom. I regularly visit that place. The helipad at Bimbat, where 'Heli Operation' was structured, is now known as 'Vijyant Helipad'. Not only that, even a road at Noida has been named as 'Captain Vijyant Thapar Marg'.

Over and above all this, he has earned a place full of love and respect in the hearts of his fellow countrymen.

Down in our memory lane, we recollected his phone call that he made from the Tololing peak through VSAT. He had told his mother over phone, "You would have already come to know by now of the heroic achievements of 2 Rajputana Rifles. We have successfully captured Tololing. Keep the newspapers of 14th, 15th and 16th June safely." He also said that he would call again after around 20 days and she should not worry about him at all. He did not tell us how fierce and dangerous that battle was—how two Pakistani soldiers at the front, when told to surrender did not lay down their arms, how they were then killed by firing from all sides, how they spent the whole night burning tin-packed butter and how they enjoyed milk maid and mixed fruits that night.

His diary had a rough sketch of that battlefield; it indicated where the bodies of Major Adhikari, Havildar, Sultan Singh and Major Gupta were lying. He was very happy with that victory and he also informed that Major Gupta would receive 'Maha Vir Chakra'. We later received a letter from him. In his conversation with his mother over phone, he had said that he would not be able to call for the next 20 days, as he was assigned another task, but he did not tell that he was chosen for one more assault that was an extremely formidable challenge namely Naul and Three Pimples. Perhaps, this was the most difficult assault that was launched on the night of 28-29th June 1999. Our country had to pay the price for the victory in the form of the martyrdom of 3 officers and 2 JCOs and injury to the two officers and 52 soldiers. Robin had led this assault operation through the medium of a narrow path. The hill was also quite steep with an inclination of around 75 degrees. The night temperature there would fall up to minus 15 degrees, and at that height of 16000 ft. where it was difficult to even breath, everybody had to carry loads of 20 to 25 kilos. Moreover, 120 mm guns and Bofors guns were aggressively pounding the area. On locating us close to them, Pakistan had also launched heavy firing. That was a full moon night. His very close friend Lance Naik Jagmal was the first to fall. They all had just got together to strike when they became the target of a Pakistani bomb. Jagmal was killed and other soldiers got injured. Robin, who was just 22 then, had to see such a close friend taking his last breath in front of him. He stood there completely lost.

- Col V N Thapar

I keep visiting Thapar Saheb's house in Noida; the Thapar family has transformed the same into a memorial. Once, I stepped into Robin's room. The items used by Robin have been safely kept there, like his uniform and his jacket that he was wearing when he exhaled his last breath. Robin's mother, Mrs Tripta Thapar told me that some dry fruits were lying in the pocket of his jacket when they got it. Ray-Ban glasses which he wore, Casio watch that he always ties around his wrist, his torch and a numerous photos and tiny statues of Lord Hanuman, everything is yet preserved in his room. Robin had deep faith in Lord Hanuman. I was flabbergasted after entering his room. Such a pure heart and the absolute devotion to the country can overwhelm anybody.

On the night of 28th June 1999, before he left for the battlefield, Robin had played Kishore Kumar's song *'Chalte chalte mere ye geet yad rakhna, Kabhi alvida na kehna...Kabhi alvida na kehna...'* on his Walkman.

The platoon set out for the battlefield after performing *pooja*-archana of Karni Mata in a traditional way and continued chanting 'Raja Ramchandra Ki Jai'.

Maj P Acharya headed to Naul. The first two bunkers were soon captured, then he lobbed hand grenades and was on the verge of overpowering the enemy in hand to hand fight when a shot hit him and he fell unconscious. On the other side, Robin along with his team lost the way and reached a spot just 100 metres from Naul. There, he came to know about Maj P Acharya's martyrdom. Hearing this news, Robin's exploded and he attacked the enemy. Making his way out of the raining bullets, he reached the enemy bunker. But just as he moved ahead for the next bunker, a bullet from the enemy's machine gun struck on his head and ended his life. It was around 2:30 am and there was only one bunker left to be captured.

The soldiers did not want the sacrifice of their two officers to go in vain. Those soldiers of the Rajputana Rifles let out a deafening chant of 'Raja Ramchandra Ki Jai' again and fell upon the enemy. Bofors guns provided ample support here and the Artillery created havoc in the enemy camp with its bombardment. Finally, the brave soldiers of Rajputana Rifles took revenge of the martyrdom of their two officers and hoisted the tricolour over Naul at 3:30 am. Without a doubt, we had to pay a heavy price for this victory.

On the other side, Captain Kenguruse was sent to capture 'Bump' in the north. The brave hearts of 2 Rajputana Rifles were ready to sacrifice everything for a victory over the enemy. It was a steep climb here and it was not easy to take steps. Kenguruse's perceived his shoes as an obstruction and he immediately removed them to make the ascent quicker. The enemy was firing indiscriminately. It is always an advantage to be positioned at a higher point and unfortunately our enemy was having this leverage. But our soldiers were in high spirits.

Despite being injured by enemy bullets, Captain Kenguruse shot two Pakistani soldiers and used his commando knife to kill another two to ensure victory for his platoon. However, he laid down his life for the country, thus maintaining the highest traditions of the Indian Army. The enemy was forced to flee. By 8 am, the entire Black Rock area was in our control and we proudly hoisted our tricolour there. Parallelly, 18 Garhwal also proved its efficacy and hoisted victory flag over Point 4700.

Brave Captain Kenguruse of 2 Rajputana Rifles was born on 15th July 1974 at Nerhema village in the Kohima District of Nagaland. During my Kohima trip in the year 2018, I was driven to visit Captain Kenguruse's village Nerhema located around 22 kilometres away from Kohima. He was posthumously awarded the 'Maha Vir Chakra' for displaying his exemplary valour in combat during the Kargil War.

Captain Kenguruse

A memorial has been built at Nerhema in the honour of Captain Kenguruse. It was my privilege to pay respect to him there. Captain Kenguruse worked as a teacher in Kohima from the years 1994 to 1997. He could have spent his life with ease and comfort in his own region, but he gave preference to serve the nation and hence joined the Army. Before leaving for the Kargil War, he got engaged to a doctor. But unfortunately, he attained martyrdom before tying the knot. His colleagues in the Regiment fondly called him as 'Nimbu Saheb'.

The day of 29th June 1999 proved to be very painful for us as we lost our 3 officers and 22 soldiers, in turn we killed 32 of enemy's soldiers. Maj P Acharya and Captain Kenguruse were honoured with the 'Maha Vir Chakra' and Captain Vijyant Thapar with 'Vir Chakra' for their exemplary valour.

On 28th June, Nawaz Sharif proceeded on his tour to China. If we believe Pakistani sources, Nawaz Sharif wanted to visit Delhi and hold a press conference along with the then Prime Minister Vajpayee to announce a ceasefire. The reason was quite significant. This would have helped him prove that he was a true politician who was there to negotiate with his neighbour for restoring peace and harmony. However, the reality was just the opposite. Firstly, by then Pakistan had got isolated in the international community, secondly it was facing heavy pressure from the United States and thirdly and the most significant reason was that—India was now having the upper hand in the war. More than half of Drās was now under India's control and it was clearly visible that Pakistan would not be able to continue its hold over remaining peaks for a longer period of time.

What Pakistan did with the bodies of its soldiers could not be hidden from the world. The soldiers who had laid down their lives for their country, were now disowned by their own countrymen. What else could be the bigger tragedy! The reason behind this action of Pakistan was to reflect on the world that they had no role in this entire war. But, by then, India had provided the ID cards of dead and few captured Pakistani soldiers on international media platforms and hence proved that the Kargil War was nothing more than a propaganda orchestrated by the Pakistan Army and the ISI. Like this, there were other umpteen evidences like Pakistani Army officers' diaries, their identity documents and their pay diaries that loudly proved them to be regular Pakistani soldiers. Salute to the spirit of the Indian Army, who for the sake of humanity, arranged the burial of those enemy soldiers with full honours. Even Pakistani flags were procured in Drās, especially for their burial. What more magnanimity we Indians could have! As such, there is a saying, children may be bad but parents are always good.

India had understood the backdoor diplomacy of Nawaz Sharif. There was no question of any compromise with the pride of the country and the sacrifice of our soldiers. At that point of time, Nawaz Sharif was so anxious about holding a press conference in Delhi that, before boarding the plane in Beijing, he even asked Brajesh Mishra,the then National Security Advisor (NSA) whether he could come to Delhi? But India had already decided its answer. Nawaz Sharif thus had to face two jolts at the same time—one from India and the other from China. China refused to offer any kind of support to him. Now all eyes turned on the then President of America, Bill Clinton. He was the only person who could rein in Pakistan and pressurise it for the declaration of a ceasefire.

❑

7

Lion of Batalik: Captain Manoj Kumar Pandey

The Indian Army, with the facilitation of its extraordinary skills, had started gaining success in the war. Our soldiers brimming with self-confidence, had decided to rest only after wiping out Pakistan. Even though many challenges were still present, we were confident to surmount them. In July 2007, when I was going from Leh to Kargil, a soldier accompanying us halted at Batalik. The Indus River crosses into Pakistan Occupied Kashmir from that area. An aesthetic view of High mountains was presented right in front of our eyes. The natural beauty was glorious. That soldier informed us that Captain Manoj Kumar Pandey, Param Vir Chakra in the Kargil war, had attained martyrdom, consequent to the encounter with enemies in that very area. It

Captain Manoj Kumar Pandey

was quite natural to remember Capt Manoj Kumar Pandey after witnessing the grand Mountains of the Batalik range. These words of Capt Manoj Kumar Pandey are still remembered, "If death strikes before I prove my blood, I promise I will kill death." And he lived up to his promise. Compared to the peaks of Drās, the terrains of Kukarthang, Jubar and Khalubar are quite inaccessible. These all are a part of the Batalik range, where Captain Manoj Kumar Pandey and his regiment, 1/11 Gorkha rifles were giving a tough time to the Pakistani Army. It was very challenging to secure victory there.

Garkhon is the location in Batalik where Pakistani infiltration was first reported to the

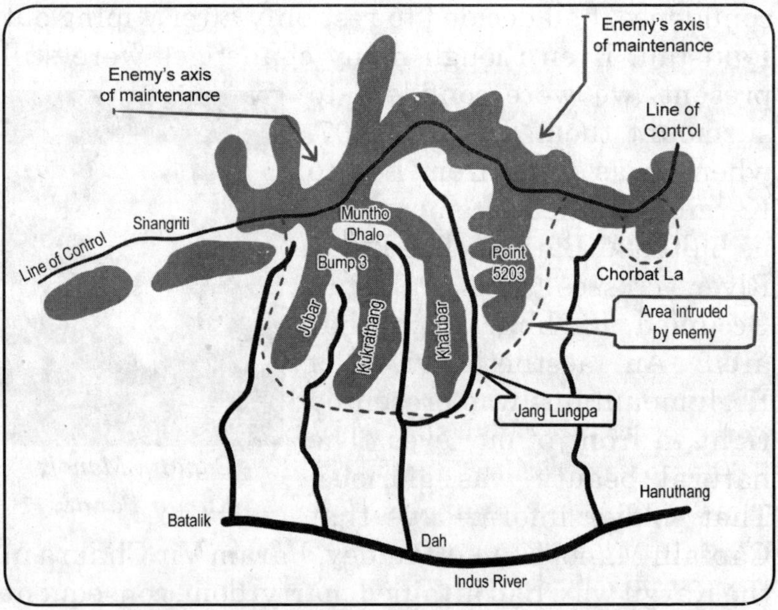

Map showing infiltration by Pakistan in Batalik sector.

Indian Army. The 3rd Punjab Regiment was deployed then.

At that time, 1/11 Gorkha Regiment had almost completed its tenure in Siachen. Capt Manoj Kumar Pandey was also scheduled to proceed on leave whenhis regiment received orders on 8th May to reach Batalik instantly. The best thing with the Gorkha Regiment was that its soldiers did not need to acclimatise as they were coming directly from the Siachen glacier area. They could straightaway go for combat. The Gorkha Regiment has a special place in the war history of India. Their indomitable courage and bravery make the Gorkha's capable of turning the tables on the enemy under any situation. The hero of year 1971, Field Marshal Manekshaw, who belonged to the Gorkha Regiment, had once commented, ***"If a man says he is not afraid of dying, he is either lying or is a Gorkha."***

It was the place named "Muntho Dhalo" in the Batalik sector, where Pakistan had set up a large administrative and logistics base. It was a kind of table top terrain, with hill on one side and ravine on the other side. This was Pakistan's largest supply route in the Kargil War. The brave soldiers of the Indian Air Force attacked Muntho Dhalo and completely wrecked the same. Pakistan had lost 160 soldiers of their army in this gruesome attack. This action of Indian Air Force severely jolted the Pakistani armed forces.

In the month of June 1999, the war was at its peak. On 30th June, 22 Grenadiers, launched strike on 'Khalubar' feature in the Batalik sector. They acquired some control there. Later, on the 2nd of July, the first regiment of 11 Gorkha Rifles was deployed there. Khalubar was divided into two parts—Khalubar South and Khalubar North, based on its geographic position. There is an area known as 'Bunker Area' right below these two peaks. Captain Manoj Kumar Pandey and his platoon was assigned the task of capturing this very area. It was 4 o'clock in the morning and was freezing out there. But, Gorkha soldiers were ready to fight to death that day. Capt Manoj Kumar Pandey assessed the situation and identified a total of six enemy bunkers that needed to be destroyed. He called Havildar Bhim Bahadur and ordered him to destroy the two bunkers on his right. He decided to carry out the job of destroying the remaining four bunkers on his left himself. Thunderous chants of 'Jai Mahakali, Aayo Gorkhali' by the Gorkha soldiers made their blood boil. The end of the enemy was looking certain. Capt Manoj, started moving ahead. He charged at the first bunker and killed two Pakistani soldiers present there.

Similarly, he killed another two Pakistanis while demolishing the second bunker. By the time he charged at the third bunker, he had already gotten injury on his leg and shoulder. But he still pressed on his solitary charge at the fourth bunker with hand grenade. At that very moment, a bullet from UMG (Universal Machine Gun) hit his face and he collapsed, laying down his life for the country. His last words before he died were 'Chhornu naheen' in

Nepalese, meaning 'Don't spare the enemy'. By 5 pm on July 3rd, the entire bunker area was under the control of Indian Army. Capt Manoj Pandey was decorated with 'Param Vir Chakra' (Posthumous) and Havildar Bhim Bahadur was honoured with 'Vir Chakra' (Posthumous) for their exemplary valour. There is no doubt that, heroes like Capt Manoj Pandey are rare.

During the month of November 2019, I was in the capital city of Uttar Pradesh, Lucknow. I contacted one of my acquaintances, Shri Madhusudan Dixit and expressed my desire to visit the parents of Capt Manoj Kumar Pandey. Fortunately, Dixit Saheb owns a school in Lucknow, where Capt Manoj Kumar Pandey had studied. He had phone number of Manoj's mother. I contacted her immediately and the very next day, I reached her house at Vishal Khand, Gomti Nagar. That was the house where Capt Manoj had spent a major portion of his life. Many pictures of his childhood were hanging on the walls there. The eldest among three brothers and one sister, Manoj was a soft-natured person. I met his mother Smt Mohini Pandey and his younger brother Shri Manmohan Pandey. They have dedicated one room of the house to the memories of Capt Manoj Pandey. Many items related to his life have been put on display there.

Born into a lower middle-class family, Capt Manoj was extraordinarily intelligent right from his childhood. After finishing his 6th and 7th standards from Rani Laxmibai School at Lucknow, he joined

Sainik School, Lucknow. This is where he developed an interest in joining the Army. Thus, he was inspired to join the Army in his childhood after watching 'Param Vir Chakra' serial, introduced by Chetan Anand in the nineteen eighties. His dreams got both the wings and direction after joining Sainik School. There, he acquired leadership skills that are expected out of an army officer. At Sainik School, he acquired

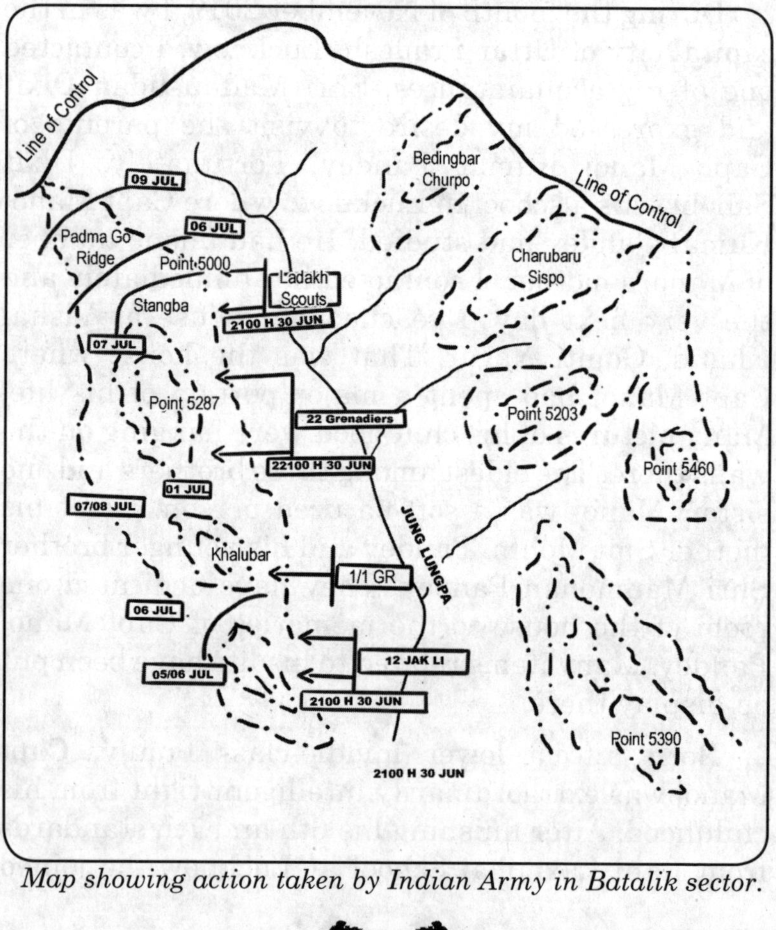

Map showing action taken by Indian Army in Batalik sector.

expertise in all the fields that could help him become a brilliant Army officer. That was the reason behind the motivation that he cleared the National Defence Academy (NDA) test in his very first attempt. He attended interview at the Service Selection Board (SSB), Varanasi, where he was asked a question, "Why do you want to join Services?" His answer was, "I want to win the Param Vir Chakra." This stunned the officers sitting in the Board. When they said that the award was usually given posthumously, Manoj, proudly responded that he was always ready to lay down his life for the nation. Who would have known that his words would become true one day?

Manoj Pandey was born in June 1975 and I was born in September 1975. Many a times, I find myself very close to his life. I had decided to join the armed services right in my 8th standard, when I joined NCC. I had even started to prepare for NDA. But it was not in my fate to serve the country as a soldier. I was selected by the Railways when I was in 10th standard, and as I belonged to a middle-class family, I had to give preference to the job over my dreams. That decision is regretted till date, for eternal. Even though, I could not wear the service uniform, I am still a soldier by heart. Meeting the family members of martyred soldiers, visiting the war zones, disseminating the stories of brave hearts to the common people and publicising them has become the primary mission of my life and I would continue doing the same till my last breath.

While looking at the photos at his Gomti Nagar residence, I was just thinking, if Manoj Pandey returned from the war that day, he would be having a family of his own today and he would have grown to be a Colonel or Brigadier by now. But fate had other plans for him. In the month of July 2018, I got an opportunity to visit the National Defence Academy, Khadakwasla, Pune; where one hall has been named after Capt Manoj Pandey.

In April 2021, I got the news that Capt Manoj Pandey's mother had left for the heavenly abode. I just could not believe that. All those moments that I had spent at their residence in November 2019 came flooding back. May the departed soul rest in peace.

Let's come back to the war zone. After the Bunker area, Khalubar South and Khalubar North were also captured on the 5th and 6th of July respectively.

After spending some time in Batalik, we reached Kargil. Our night stay was arranged at the Army Guest House. A board on the NH 1 near Harka Bahadur Bridge at Kargil had the following warning, "Beware! The enemy is watching you!" We were also accompanied by a friend who worked for the local administration at Kargil. He informed us that a Pakistan post was located at a distance of just 5 kilometres from there and they could watch us from that post and even fire on us. For that very reason, a wall has been erected there to protect NH 1D from the enemy. Our friend at last asked us,"Would you like to see the post?" We responded in the affirmative. That road goes towards Skardu in Pakistan Occupied Kashmir.

It was the Shingo River flowing on our left. In fact, the Drās River that comes from Drās joins the Shingo River at Kaksar which comes from Pakistan. This river then becomes 'Shingo'. The Suru River, originating in Jhanskar in Kargil joins the Vaka Rong River in Kargil but retains its name as Suru. Later, Suru and Shingo rivers merge near the Harka Bahadur Bridge and flow as Shingo towards Skardu in Pakistan. A little further down i.e., just after crossing the Line of Control, the Shingo River joins the Indus River at Marol village and then onwards, it's known as the Indus only. I have already mentioned this in detail earlier. We reached the last village close to the LOC in just 20 minutes. But the view there was quite picturesque. Right in front of us was the Pakistan post from where they were keeping a watch over our National Highway.

We returned to our Guest House shortly thereafter. I had met Colonel Gehlot in Kargil during an evening in the year 2007. Hailing from Rajasthan, Col Gehlot appeared to be a fun-loving person. He arranged our visit to the Kala Pahad Post. The Kala Pahad Post is the last post on the Line of Control and the Pakistan territory starts from there. It was pleasing to find that TV and dish antenna had been installed there for our soldiers. We would never forget the thrill of viewing the Line of Control while enjoying tea and hot *pakodas*.

There was a flag flying over there with 'Om' on one side and a picture of Lord Hanuman on the other side. On enquiry, we learnt that this flag is installed at all the forward Indian posts. Indian soldiers are extremely religious. The religious unity of the Army is well known. Whatever be the religion, everybody in the Army has only one goal—India's victory at any cost! We did see many such examples during the Kargil War. During that war, the soldiers of Rajputana Rifles and Jammu & Kashmir Rifles were seen making their war cry 'Raja Ramchandra ki Jai' and 'Durga Mata ki Jai'. The soldiers of Sikh Regiment and Punjab Regiment were seen chanting 'Bole So Nihal, Sat Shri Akal' whereas 1 Naga soldiers, most of them belonging to Christian community of Nagaland, were praying in accordance with their religion. The point to be noted is that they all pray to God collectively. The same priest who was a little while ago helping others chant mantras and perform pooja, was later found to be armed with gun and participating in combat. Such a tradition and religious unity can be found only in the Indian Army.

Very soon, we returned to the mess and freshened up. I still remember the movie 'Don-2' was being telecasted on TV that day. We went out for a stroll after dinner. I just thought of calling somebody but my mobile was not getting any signal. I came to know that there was only one mobile tower belonging to BSNL in the area and that was also not working since the last one week. I was advised to use a PCO booth; and I readily agreed. Otherwise, I had no other option. I reached the PCO booth where some servicemen were already waiting for their turn. I also waited for 10 minutes and then enjoyed the pleasure of calling from a PCO booth after so many years. In a way, I was feeling happy that my mobile didn't work—no phone, no tension and hence no worries! I believe that even today, use of mobile phones appear to me as constraint on our freedom. Anybody can call anytime even if you are not willing to talk. Over and above that, marketing calls make it even worse. Believe me, in the present age, if I go somewhere and mobile does not work, I feel so relieved.

While waiting in the queue for the phone, I was thinking of the situation during the Kargil War. There was only one PCO booth in Drās. There used to be long queues of anxious soldiers waiting to talk to their family members. Some of them might have returned from war zones while some others might be preparing to go next day. They all must have been just desperate to talk to their families once. As a result, whenever the phone went out of order, which did happen quite often, many of the soldiers would be dejected. Many a times, the satellite phone of the Army would come as a big relief. Lt Col Vishwanathan of 18 Grenadiers wanted to talk to his family before leaving for the Tololing mission. Satellite phone was arranged from the base station only for him but unfortunately, its battery was not working and he left for the mission without making the call and could not return alive. Such things do happen in life.

The next morning, we went to see Complex 43. This complex is situated on the LOC from where Pakistani soldiers can be seen manning their posts. On-duty soldiers told us that the spot where we were standing was earlier occupied by Pakistan. Our National Highway going to Leh was just in front of us. Earlier, we had to take permission from the Pakistani officials every time we had to take a vehicle across this spot, and that was quite awkward. After the war in the year 1971, we moved ahead a little and acquired complex 43 from Pakistan, thus this problem was solved forever. Technically then, we had no control but the Pakistan Occupied Kashmir belongs to us. Now, after the division of Jammu & Kashmir and abrogation of Article 370, our next target that was and till date is to acquire control over POK back to India. We got excited to see the milestone there with inscription as 'POK, i.e., Pakistan Occupied Kashmir, 600 Meters'. Just next to that was a Pakistan flag post. A Pakistani soldier came out in tracksuit and after looking at us, went inside.

This place had turned quite significant and sensitive during the Kargil War. This was the place where Pakistan Army had handed over the bodies of some of our soldiers. I just recollected the names of Sqn Ldr Ajay Ahuja and Lt Saurabh Kalia whose bodies were handed over to us at this very spot. The way Pakistan killed them was a disgrace to humanity. All this made me emotional. That day, when Sqn Ldr Ajay Ahuja took off for the last time during the Kargil War, he had Rs 1500 in his pocket, meant for booking air tickets for his wife and son. But fate had some other plans. When Pakistan handed over his body to India, they also handed over that envelope with the same Rs 1500 in it.

What Pakistan did with Lt Saurabh Kalia could not be termed anything less than a heinous crime. It was difficult to imagine that Pakistan would breach all the limits of humanity like that. Lt Saurabh Kalia's father was so hurt by the incident that he even wrote a letter to then Pakistan's Prime Minister Nawaz Sharif; the letter clearly reflects a father's pain and distress for his son. He wrote:

Addressed to: primeminister@pak.gov.pk
Class 2/3: Request and Complaint
The Prime Minister
Islamic Republic of Pakistan

Sir,

I am the proud father of Shaheed Lt Saurabh Kalia of the Indian Army who laid down his life for the nation while doing duty of guarding the frontiers of Kargil.

Pakistan had captured alive the patrol party comprising him and five other brave soldiers. They were in your custody for three weeks and were subjected to countless inhuman tortures, as evident from their bodies handed over by the Pakistan Army. They didn't break even after that endless barbarity. This speaks a lot about their patriotism, determination and bravery and the entire country is proud of them.

Pakistan has committed infringement on the following counts:

1. They were captured alive, but Indian counterparts were not informed of their POW status.

2. They were subjected to torture never seen before and that was in violation of the Geneva Convention.

Through this letter, I would like to raise following points in respect of the heinous and inhuman treatment meted out to those soldiers:

1. Every soldier of a disciplined army fight for his motherland and if he makes the supreme sacrifice in the course of his duty, nobody should regret the same.

2. In a war, taking prisoner or getting imprisoned is its part; despite that, people in your country indulged in dastardly acts of burning bodies with cigarettes, removing eyes and chopping of various limbs and subjecting them to unimaginable tortures. They were shot dead ultimately. This would traumatise anybody and overwhelm them with intolerable pain. May I pose some questions for those culprits who committed those crimes? Are they not humans? Don't they have children? Does your country follow the law of the jungle? Does your culture teach you to treat a human, which is a wonderful creation of God, like this? If yes, then this surely is a blemish. I pray Allah curses all those heartless culprits who have committed such an unpardonable crime. If my prayer is pure and coming from my heart, they would surely face Allah's wrath.

Try to learn from India at least. When India took around 93,000 Pakistanis as prisoners of war in the year 1971, they were set free unharmed in in the year 1972. We returned all 93,000 prisoners of war to you safe and sound. It's a request to you—go and ask those soldiers and their families how they felt when they met after that separation. Pakistan would have been in deep turmoil had they not returned safely to their homes. Please go and ask those soldiers how they were treated here.

I fail to understand how your government could wash its hand of this barbaric act by claiming that infiltrators committed this heinous crime. I am not an expert on political and military affairs to comment on the war; but as the father of my son, I appeal for immediate filing of case against the perpetrators of this immoral act and bringing them to justice. Your army must be aware of the persons who had handed over the bodies of these soldiers to them.

I also request you to find out the date on which they were shot dead so that we celebrate that day every year as 'Shaheed Diwas'. That would be your personal obligation to the undersigned.

Thanking you,

Yours truly

- Dr N K Kalia

In April 2019, I got an opportunity to visit the parents of brave Captain Saurabh Kalia at Palampur in Himachal Pradesh. For sure, Saurabh had not revealed the information that Pakistanis were looking for and perhaps that was the reason they did everything possible to torture him. One room at the residence of Saurabh Kalia has been converted into a museum in his memory; his uniform, some old photographs, some personal effects and most importantly, a pot containing the soil of that pious land of the Bajrang Post where Saurabh was deployed is also preserved.

The pain of losing their son under these circumstances was quite apparent in the eyes of Saurabh Kalia's father, Dr Narendra Kumar Kalia and his mother Smt Vijaya Kalia. Saurabh's mother had suffered a heart attack on hearing the news that her son was missing. She even resigned from her government job after Saurabh's martyrdom. She showed me the State Bank of India cheque book that Saurabh had given her before going to war. With tears in her eyes, she said that Saurabh had told her to withdraw money whenever she required. But fate had other plans.

Even before the first salary was paid, after his posting, he attained martyrdom.

After the Kargil War, The Chief of Army Staff visited their house. His father has not been able to forget the inhuman treatment meted out to Saurabh. How can a father forget such a devastating pain? Dr Narendra Kalia is striving for justice for the last two decades after the Kargil War. He has been constantly making efforts to secure justice for Saurabh Kalia by taking Pakistan to the International Court. Dr Kalia is fighting his case in the Supreme Court. He has made this case the mission of his life.

After that meeting, I am in constant touch with Saurabh's brother Vaibhav Kalia. During a chat, he told me how Saurabh and he would take rounds of Palampur cantonment on a motorcycle. Saurabh had great love and respect for the Army. He also briefed that after Saurabh's body was brought to Palampur, he had gone to the cantonment for the identification of the body. *Saurabh's face had nothing left except his eyebrows.* My heart ached with pain on hearing this. How can a family live in comfort when their young child had endured the pain beyond all limits? However, one thing that consoles me a bit is the fact that people from all parts of the country keep visiting the Kalia family even today. There are many people who keep encouraging Dr Kalia even today, extending their support until Saurabh gets justice.

❑

8

Pride of India: Tiger Hill

Immediately after I reached Drās with my group, in the year 2007, we were taken to Sando Top. This was the site of a fierce battle ground during the Kargil War. There is a viewing gallery where families of the martyrs of the Kargil War are briefed about the war and Tiger Hill is shown to them. Besides this, they are also apprised of other significant peaks that were nearly impossible to capture. Still, our valiant soldiers not only got them back safely from Pakistan, but also taught them a lifelong lesson that would restrain them from indulging in such audacity again in the future. We felt immensely proud to know all this.

Our soldiers were in great spirits after their victory over Tololing, Point 5140 and some other major peaks. On 3rd July, regaining Tiger Hill at any cost was decided as the next major mission. Tiger Hill is the symbol of our pride and self- esteem. The exquisiteness of Tiger Hill looks astounding from the Srinagar-Kargil highway NH-1D. The height of 16,500 ft. provides it with a unique magnificence. It

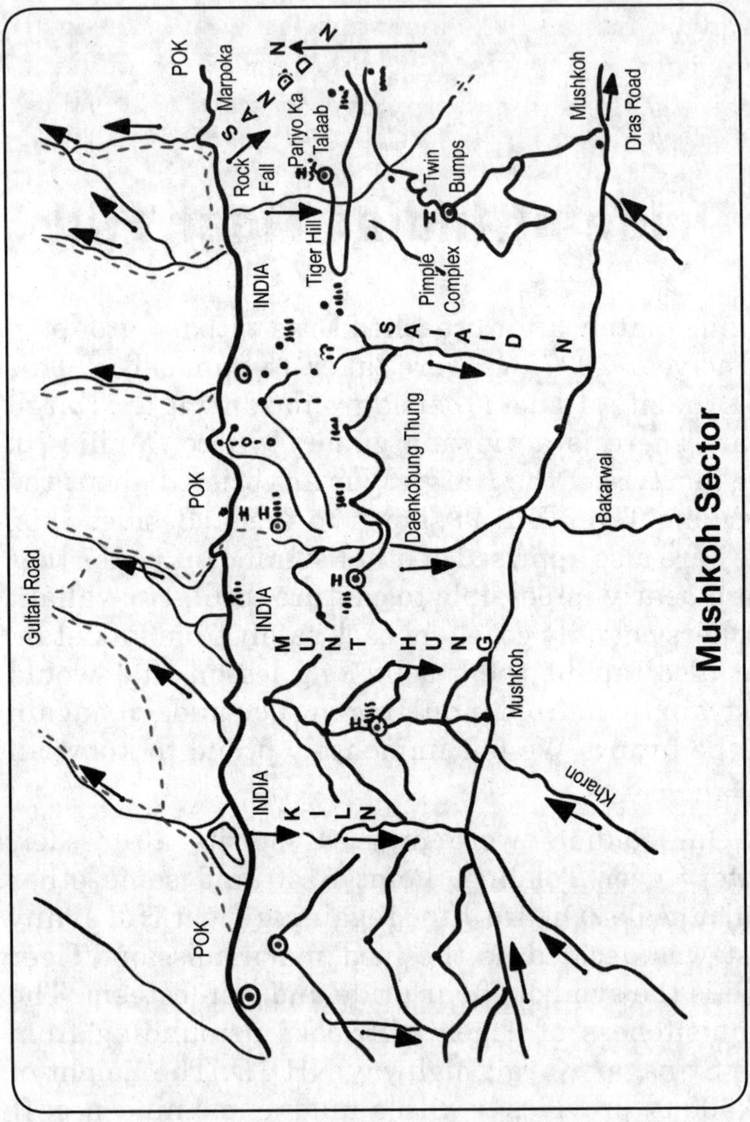

Map showing Tiger Hill and Mushkoh Valley

was difficult to take our eyes off the Hill. Its natural beauty is mesmerizing. The month of July 1999 was already scary, and the fact that Tiger Hill was still encroached by Pakistan, bothered every Indian. Regaining the same at any cost was the only thing that could provide solace to us. Every child in the country was aware of Tiger Hill; this made it all the more important to secure a victory over it. For a common Indian, if there was any other peak more significant after Tololing, it was Tiger Hill. Even this was known to the enemy. We were fully aware that the enemy would use all its power to retain this peak. On 24th June 1999, Brigadier M. P. S. Bajwa of 192 Mountain Brigade issued an order to regain Tiger Hill after devising a proper strategy. 18 Grenadiers and 8 Sikh immediately started preparing the plans to capture the peak.

On that night of 3rd July, when the fight for the nation's pride was to take place, the Indian Army was ceaselessly regaining all the areas from the Pakistan Army one by one. Brave soldiers of the Ghatak platoon of 18 Grenadiers were advancing up the mountain to accomplish the impossible task of capturing Tiger Hill. Besides this, 2 Naga and 8 Sikh were assigned the task of capturing the western pass of Tiger Hill covering areas like India Gate and Helmet. Any mistake could have proved fatal. We needed to ensure best strategy. It was decided that 18 Grenadiers would launch an attack on Tiger Hill from three sides and brave commandos of the

Ghatak platoon, led by Lt Balwan Singh, would advance up the mountain from northeast side.

19-year-old Subedar Yogendra Singh Yadav was accompanying them. (He has been super-annuated in 2021 from the post of Honorary Captain). The decision to launch an attack from this side could have surprised anybody, as it was almost a vertical cliff with a gradient of approximately 90 degrees. Pakistan could not have ever expected a strike from this side. The second platoon led by Lt Sachin Nimbalkar was to advance up from the southern end of Tiger Hill. Even they didn't know that how the situation would turn, and both the teams at different ends will launch a collective attack to ensure victory.

Capt. Yogendra Singh Yadav

It was chilling cold that day. Chasing off the enemy in that temperature of almost 15 degrees below zero, that too when the enemy was positioned at a higher point was not easy. At this situation, one enemy soldier sitting at a higher point is equivalent to ten soldiers at the ground level. To fight and secure victory in such circumstances was nothing less than a miracle. But, the brave soldiers of the Indian Army are capable of making impossible possible. God was on our side on that night of 3rd July, as the weather was fully supporting us. It was a cloudy and dark night. The enemy was not in a position to spot us from a distance.

The Artillery again played a key role in the victory over Tiger Hill. In addition to that, the fighter planes of the Air Force used laser bombs to break the enemy's back. Bombardments at that spot had already been initiated on 2nd July. Lt (now Colonel) Balwan Singh, instead of carrying his foodstuff, packed an equivalent weight of bullets. He was desperate to pump those bullets in the enemy's chest. They started the ascent. 19-year-old Yogendra Singh would first lob the rope, hang on the same to make sure it was strong enough and then help his men to climb up. Belonging to Bulandshahar in Uttar Pradesh, Yogendra was newly married. Just after the marriage function was over, he had received the order to report for the war.

Colonel Balwan Singh

Just before reaching the top, clouds suddenly opened up and the enemy got a sight of our team. The firing started. Two bullets also hit Lt Balwan Singh. But he still refused to leave the ground. He kept on boosting the morale of his men and stood

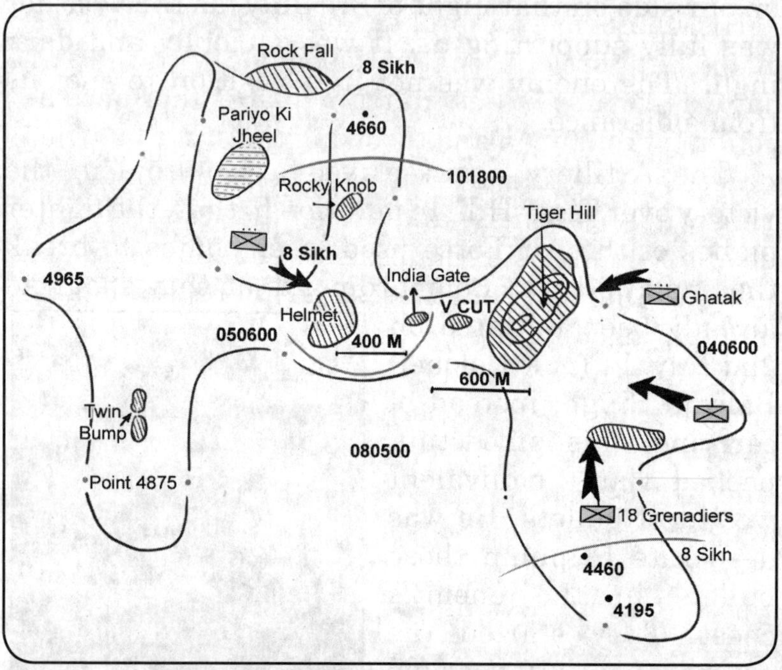

Map showing operations of the Indian Army in the Tiger Hill Battlefield

there firm. Subedar Yogendra Singh was already hit by 17 bullets, but he was still in high spirits and continued chanting 'Bharat Mata Ki Jai'. That invincible courage and unflinching determination at that tender age of 19 could be a God given gift only. Subedar Yogendra Singh's father has also been a serviceman. Yogendra had heard many stories in his childhood about the bravery of the soldiers. That day, he had one and only one mission—to hoist the tricolour over Tiger Hill. He destroyed the first two bunkers. But the enemy was still raining bullets on him; a grenade exploded on his face, almost blinding him.

His one arm was broken and hanging. He was unable to figure out what is to be done with the arm that was torn by bullets in many places. For once he thought of removing and throwing the same but then he tied the hanging arm with his belt and continued firing with his other hand. Yogendra was the only one alive among his remaining seven fellow soldiers. Meanwhile, he noticed that some more Pakistanis were approaching, he pretended to be a dead body. But Pakistanis wanted to ensure that none of the Indian soldiers lying there were alive. The enemy soldiers came and fired indiscriminately. Some bullets hit Yogendra's legs but he lay quietly. And then, a bullet hit his chest. Thanks to the Five(5) rupee coin that was there in his wallet kept in the upper pocket of his uniform, it took the hit on itself and saved Yogendra's life. However, the impact was so hard that it made Yogendra assume that he was dead. Just then, a Pakistani soldier's foot hit his leg; it generated a sensation and he was convinced that he was alive. Yogendra then said to himself, if he had not lost his life even after so much, he was not going to lose the same anyway! a thriving soldier indeed.

He remembered God and lobbed a grenade towards the Pakistani soldier standing in front of him. The grenade got caught in the hood of the soldier's jacket behind his head and when he tried to remove the same, it blasted and he was killed. Yogendra then picked a Pika gun of the enemy and, hiding behind different rocks in turn, started firing. The enemy thought the assault was re-launched. This wreaked havoc in the enemy's camp. By then, Yogendra had killed 9 enemy soldiers. The remaining Pakistani soldiers fled away. Yogendra took courage and inspected the enemy camp. And then, though severely injured, he decided to make his fellow soldiers aware of the enemy's strike plan that he had overheard while lying down there. He didn't want them to fall into the enemy's trap and lose their lives. He decided to let his fellow soldiers have this information at any cost and pushed himself into a stream flowing close by. He managed to flow with the stream down. For once, he thought he was in the enemy territory. But his apprehension proved to be wrong when he saw his fellow soldiers there; he immediately told them about the enemy's plot and thus ensured the safety of many valuable lives. By this time, he had already lost a lot of blood, was losing consciousness and his sight was almost gone. He was immediately taken to base camp and provided warmth with the help of 4-5 stoves and blankets. Once his body was a bit warm, Yogendra narrated the entire story to his Commanding Officer Col Khushal Singh; he was then transferred to a hospital. It was not an ordinary valour to wreak such havoc in the enemy camp braving adverse circumstances, that also when his officer was not accompanying him and he was taking all decisions on his own at the age of just 19 years. Undoubtedly, this was a demonstration of exceptional valour. On account of a mistake by a clerk of the Northern Command, he was declared martyred. There, he came to know that his namesake and also a close friend (his name was also Subedar Yogendra Singh Yadav) were to be given 'Param Vir Chakra'. He must have surely felt happy when the then Chief of Army Staff informed him later that it was not his friend but him only who going to be awarded 'Param Vir Chakra'. Subedar Yogendra Singh Yadav was awarded 'Param Vir Chakra' for displaying the most conspicuous courage and indomitable gallantry. Aged 19 when he received the decoration, he was the youngest soldier to be awarded Param Vir Chakra.

22-year-old 2nd Lt Arun Khetrapal previously held this honour; he had received this decoration for his bravery during the 1971 India-Pakistan war. On the occasion of the Independence Day of the year 2021, Yogendra Singh Yadav was conferred the rank of 'Honorary Captain' that he amply deserved.

I keep meeting Captain Yogendra Singh Yadav quite often. Every meeting with him has been a source of inspiration for me. I feel as if he is a superhuman who was chosen by God himself for annihilation of the enemy in the Kargil war. Even after taking 17 bullets into his body, the only thought that preoccupied his mind at that point of time was to somehow defeat the enemy. He can't be a normal human. It was no less than a miracle that his body withstood so many bullets.

Lt Balwan Singh also, by dicing with death that day, demonstrated that the lives of his fellow soldiers were more valuable than his own life and the security of the country was more important than his own safety. Hailing from Jhajjar in Haryana, Balwan Singh belonged to an ordinary family. His father also was a serviceman and hence, he had also inherited patriotism. He knew that the fight that day was not an ordinary fight, instead, it was a fight for honour and every soldier of the Indian Army was ready to lay down his life for the same. He demonstrated exceptional leadership skills. He was honoured with 'Maha Vir Chakra' for his conspicuous courage and exceptional bravery. He along with his fellow soldiers attained victory in this extremely important war and hoisted the tricolour over Tiger Hill.

In year 2019, I got an opportunity to meet this brave heart at his Panchkula residence. I was yearning to shake hands with such a hero who had killed innumerable enemy soldiers in the Kargil War with the same hands. Lt Balwan Singh is since promoted to Colonel. Since then talks about his old days brings a smile to his face and a unique shine in his eyes. During our talk, he narrated what happened in the war on that momentous day, how it all happened and how our perfect strategy compelled the enemy to flee from Tiger Hill. His son studying in the 12th standard is very impressed by his father's valorous life and he also wants to follow in the footsteps of his father and join the Army. The lives of all the heroes who fought the Kargil War and demolished the enemy with their bravery are not just simple lives but have turned into sagas. These brave hearts are the real heroes of our society. The stories of their bravery should get disseminated to every youth in every house; that would inspire the youth to do for their society and the country something that would be remembered for ages. In fact, instead of ages, it would be apt to say the sagas of these heroes would remain in the heart of every Indian so long as the sun shines.

The story of the victory of Tiger Hill would be incomplete without the mention of 8th Battalion of the Sikh Regiment. The task of securing victory over southern and western parts of Tiger Hill, which was divided into several parts like India Gate, Rocky Knob and Helmet, was assigned to 8 Sikh. Major Sherawat and Major Parmar were in command. Maj Parmar, along with Subedar Nirmal Singh, disconnected phone lines of the enemy at India Gate. 8 Sikh did something unique; It used several megaphones (used for making announcements). The soldiers would intermittently chant 'Jo Bole So Nihal, Sat Sri Akal' with full vigour. The echoes of those chants coming back from the rocks would give an impression of thousands of soldiers marching together towards Tiger Hill. All this made the enemy shiver in fear. It thought that India had deployed a full brigade for the attack that day. 8 Sikh very efficiently executed

Subedar Nirmal Singh

the job of misleading the enemy by creating confusion; this was done to help 18 Grenadiers launching an attack from the other side. And that is what happened; the strategy of the Army worked. 8 Sikh was primarily responsible for capturing India Gate and Helmet. In order to boost their morale, Brigade Commander Barar prompted them to recollect the battle of Saragarhi where 21 Sikhs had turned the tables and attained victory. Subedar Nirmal Singh, Naib Subedar Karnail Singh and Sepoy Satpal Singh of 8 Sikh were awarded 'Vir Chakra'.

Finally, India emerged as victors. However, it was a war of honour for Pakistan also. Its supply line, which was coming from Gultari on the other side of the border, was still active and uninterrupted. It was imperative for India to break this supply line in order to ensure victory. Gultari is a cantonment of the Pakistan Army in Pakistan Occupied Kashmir. It is quite close to the Line of Control. Their soldiers would get killed but promptly replaced. This continued for three days. The Indian soldiers led by Brigade Commander M. P. S. Bara were determined not to let Pakistan return to Tiger Hill at any cost. Finally, the entire Tiger Hill was under our control on 8 July 1999. When the sangars were inspected after capture, they looked unbelievable. Three light infantry guns weighing around 1000 kilograms were also recovered from the sangars; they could not have been transported there without the use of helicopters. All this cleared many of our doubts.

It becomes necessary to mention the name of Major Chandrabhushan Dwivedi when we talk of

Major Chandrabhushan Dwivedi

the Artillery. Maj Dwivedi's regiment 315 Field Regiment was deployed in Kargil on 14 May 1999. Our soldiers had to make strenuous efforts due to adverse geographic conditions, but the enemy was challenged powerfully. Maj Dwivedi and his fellow soldiers fought with great bravery and played significant role in India's victory over Tiger Hill and Point 4875 by 2 July. They gave their best for the country during the toughest period of the war. They would keep pounding the enemy with their guns for hours to provide vital support to our soldiers who were launching assaults by climbing up the hills.

As I have mentioned earlier, Pakistan possessed a Weapon Locating Radar that helped their soldiers in detecting and locating enemy Artillery units. To avoid getting detected and hit by return firing, our soldiers had to promptly relocate the guns left or right after firing. During a similar exercise, Maj Dwivedi got hit by enemy fire and lost his life. He was posthumously awarded, Sena Medal. Maj Dwivedi's wife Mrs Bhavna Dwivedi lives in Dwarka, New Delhi and is a mother of two talented daughters. Her daughter Deeksha has written a book having a collection of letters which were written from war zones by the bravehearts who attained martyrdom during the Kargil war; the book is full of emotions. Her second daughter, Neha Dwivedi has co-authored the biography of Kargil hero Captain Vijyant Thapar with his father Col Thapar.

After the briefing on Sando Top, we returned to 'Tiger Hill' base for lunch. All the four chairs were taken out of the jeep. We had *pulao* for lunch. While having lunch, Maj Singh made us aware of quite a few other details. After lunch, we started for Mushkoh valley, the most beautiful place in that area. This valley was much in the news during the Kargil War. A victory over Point 4875, now known as 'Batra Top', would have given us control over the entire Drās. The area from Point 4875 to Ghumri came within the firing range of Pakistan. Hence, it was very important to capture the same. However, priority-wise it was first Tololing, then Tiger Hill and after that Drās—everything was going as per our plan.

❑

9

Heavenly Beauty: Mushkoh Valley

After travelling around 4 kilometres along a narrow road running on the right of Drās- Srinagar Road, we reached a beautiful valley welcoming us with open arms. That was "Mushkoh". Our driver parked the car next to a Nallah (Small stream is known as Nallah in Kargil area). The Nallah was flowing with perfectly clear water and a part of the same was covered with ice. We were standing there on 6 July 2007, and if I take you 8 years back i.e., in 1999, the same spot was witnessing a massive action.

India had already launched an assault on Point 4875. Captain Anuj Nayyar, Captain Vikram Batra and hundreds of soldiers like them were getting ready to lay down their lives for the pride of India. However, India did attain victory in the war but it had to pay a huge price for the same. That price was the lives of Captain Vikram Batra and Captain Anuj Nayyar and many other brave hearts. Traversing through the middle of two big mountains, Mushkoh

Nallah later merges with Drās Nallah. For long, this has been a safe passage for infiltration from Pakistan to India. This route has been used for years. At the time of the war, there were only 53 houses with around 450 residents in Mushkoh valley. A diary recovered from a Pakistani soldier during the war revealed that the then Pakistan Army Chief General Pervez Musharraf had visited Mushkoh during February 1999 to review the preparations of the Pakistan Army. He had even given sweets worth Rs 8000 for his soldiers. The presence of the chief of enemy army in our territory demonstrated their fearless intents. Despite that, our army ruined all their evil plans.

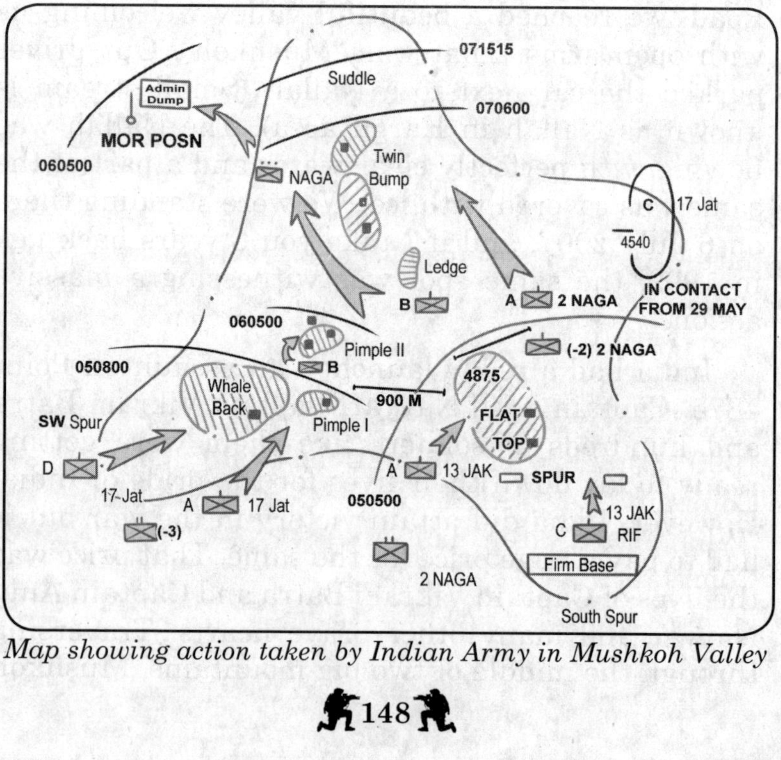

Map showing action taken by Indian Army in Mushkoh Valley

The well-built and tall young army officer with an ever-present smile on his face was none other than Captain Anuj Nayyar. This officer belonging to 17 Jat Regiment was brave and fearless right from his childhood. He got engaged just a few days before joining the Kargil War.

Captain Anuj Nayyar

His fiancé was his schoolmate and both were in friendship for the last 10 years. She was related to an army family. They were scheduled to get married on 10 September 1999. Anuj was the first in his family to join the Indian Army. His brother reveals that he was selected for three premier institutions—first the Indian Army, second NIFT (National Institute of Fashion Technology) and third, Hotel Management. He could have chosen a comfortable profession, but as per his nature, he chose the most challenging job i.e., the Indian Army.

The enemy was positioned on the vertical slope of the Pimple Complex at the height of 16000 ft. It was very difficult to attack them. On 5th July 1999, Commander Major Deepak Rampal of Delta Company was assigned the task of capturing the "Whale Back" area. This area is a part of the Pimple Complex.

They were running short of ammunition. Commanding Officer Col Umesh Singh Bawa of 17

Jat deputed the Charlie Company of Captain Anuj Nayyar for helping Major Rampal. Col Bawa, who belongs to Delhi, addressed his soldiers to lift their spirits, "Only fortunate ones get the chance to go to a war. You all have got this chance to do something for your country; go ahead and prove yourself." Before setting out for the attack, Anuj handed over his engagement ring and watch to his CO Col Bawa, however, he wanted him to wear them, as they could inspire him. But Anuj probably had something else in his mind.

The Whale Back is another historic feature, which was captured by India initially. However, Pakistan attacked Whale Back three times but faced defeat every single time. Finally, Capt Anuj Nayyar and Maj Deepak Rampal hoisted the tricolour over Whale Back. On 6th July, Capt Anuj Nayyar was assigned the task to capture Pimple II located in the same area on the western slopes of Point 4875. This area was a part of the Pimple Complex. The Company Commander Maj Ritesh Sharma got injured and had to return to the base camp.

The command then devolved upon a 24-year-old brave heart Capt Anuj Nayyar. Anuj demonstrated unprecedented leadership skills during the assault. This hero bravely led from the front and after stopping all his fellow soldiers, took just one soldier with him and slowly crawled ahead on his hands and legs and very quietly reached just below the enemy sangar. He lobbed a hand grenade inside the sangar. Demonstrating his indomitable courage and unprecedented valour, he killed 9 Pakistani soldiers and destroyed their three bunkers. While clearing the fourth bunker, an RPG (Rocket Propelled Grenade) hit him directly on his neck, resulting in his death instantly. At 5:50 am, 7th July, Col Bawa tried to contact Anuj's team over the radio set but did not get any answer. He asked Maj Punia who was on a nearby peak to have a look. At 7:30 am, Maj Punia found Anuj's body on Pimple II and informed Commanding Officer Col Bawa. The brave heart Capt Anuj Nayyar was no more. Whale Back, Pimple I and Pimple II proved to be quite challenging for 17 Jat. We did attain victory but had to pay a big price. We had to lose 1 Captain, 1 JCO and 34 other soldiers in this operation.

Captain Anuj Nayyar was awarded 'Maha Vir Chakra' (Posthumous) for his indomitable courage and unprecedented valour. Col Bawa, Maj Deepak Rampal, Captain Ghildiyal and Havildar Kumar Singh were awarded 'Vir Chakra'.

In Mushkoh valley, we were standing on the spot where Capt Anuj Nayyar had attained martyrdom. A small temple has been built there in the memory of these martyrs. I was just thinking, had my dream of joining the Army after NDA come true, possibly I also would have got the opportunity to make the supreme sacrifice for my country. However, not everybody is fortunate enough to get that opportunity. Everybody is destined to die one day, but only a few lucky ones become immortal. Capt Anuj Nayyar was one of those fortunate martyrs who had the blessings of God. He became immortal and would be in our memories forever. Till now, I have got opportunities to touch the feet of Capt Anuj Nayyar's mother Smt Meena Nayyar five-six times. I find myself to be quite close to Capt Anuj Nayyar. There is a difference of just one week between our ages. However, now he would be 24 forever. But yes, so long as the Sun and the Moon go around, the world would remember him, salute him and remain indebted to him for his sacrifice.

Anuj studied in the Army Public School at Dhaula Kuan, Delhi during his childhood. Nayyar family stayed in Janakpuri area, West Delhi at that time. Anuj's father was a lecturer in the North Campus of Delhi University and his mother a librarian in the South Campus. Everybody would wonder how this family with academic interests got somebody having interest in guns. Meena aunty told me that Anuj was self-willed right from his childhood. He would do whatever he wanted. He was also fearless and brave; in other words, he had all the qualities expected out of an army officer. He was once asked why he wanted to join the army. His answer was quite simple, he wanted to go to Siachen and find out who was stronger— he or Siachen. Anuj didn't hide anything from his father. Father and son had a friendly relationship. Anuj's father taught him to always remember three things—first, never to show his back in a battlefield, second, never to take a hit on his back and third, always teach his enemy a lesson. As an obedient son, he followed all the three lessons literally and obediently. He wrote a letter to his father from the battlefield. It was as follows:

22 June 1999

Dear Dad,

Got your inspiring letter on 14th June. Don't worry. I am yet to face an opponent who can defeat me. That day can never come when I have to admit defeat. Fear was never in the dictionary you gave me as my Dad. Well, you are 200% right, the ground air never hides anything. I've honed up my skill in the art of fighting with weapons, knives and bare hands too. Don't worry because nothing ever worries your son. Just worried about you five (Mom, You, Kannu, Timmy and Naughty). Take care of yourself and my gentleman & officer's promise, will celebrate your 25th anniversary in August.

Dad, take care of Mom. I know she worries a lot. You too must be getting solid kicks for letting me join the Army. Worry not. Your son is on your side always although I can't take your side openly against Mom. Bhai, she is head of our family na!!

Gotta go. Take care & keep smiling. It always makes me smile.

Love, Anuj

Brave hearts like Anuj are rare. I follow Meena aunty on Facebook and Twitter. I feel very happy to see that Anuj's close friends, even after a lapse of 22 years, keep visiting Meena aunty on regular basis and pay homage to Anuj. Now, she manages a petrol pump at Kondli (near Mayur Vihar) in Delhi.

The government had allotted this pump to her after Anuj Nayyar's sacrifice. A road in Janakpuri area of South-West Delhi, where Anuj once lived, has been named as 'Captain Anuj Nayyar Marg'.

Let's go back to the war zone where Captain Singh showed us Point 4875 i.e., Batra Top. This peak was very significant, as some 30-kilometre-long section of our National Highway was coming under the firing range of the enemy from this point. The peaks here were even more dangerous, deserted and frightening compared to the near by peaks in the region.

The joint responsibility of launching an assault on Point 4875 was assigned to 2 Naga, 13 JAK Rif and 17 Jat. 2 Naga captured the peak named Twin Bump and then 13 JAK Rif was assigned the task of capturing Point 4875. 13 Jammu & Kashmir Rifles was in high spirits after its victory over Point 5140. Its soldiers led by Lt Col Joshi were giving a tough fight to Pakistan. 13 JAK Rif had attained control over Point 4875 by 13th July. But Pakistan was repeatedly coming back to strike. Hence, Captain Batra was planning to go to Point 4875 at midnight of 6th July to help his fellow soldiers. He was running a high fever then, but a chant of 'Maa Durga' miraculously infused some divine power in his body and he set out to confront the enemy. The news that Vikram Batra himself was coming to help them also boosted the morale of the soldiers already fighting at higher points and they all organised with fresh enthusiasm to tear apart the enemy. Mushkoh valley was having severe cold weather on 6th and 7th July and light snowfall also started.

With the speed of a cheetah, Vikram joined his fellow soldiers promptly and attacked the enemy with his AK 47 rifle. He killed 5 Pakistanis in a face to face combat; but while trying to save his fellow soldier Lt Naveen Anaberu who was severely injured, he was hit by a bullet in his chest. He collapsed and succumbed to his injuries. In fact, a Subedar of his Battalion first came forward to save Lt Naveen Anaberu but Captain Batra stopped him saying, "You step back, you have a family." *The leadership character that he demonstrated there is rarely found in the history*. The last words spoken by Captain Batra were 'Jai Mata Di'. Vikram's sacrifice enraged all the Indian soldiers present there and they all, without caring for their lives, fell on the enemy and drove it away from there.

Subedar Sanjay Kumar

The flat top area of Point 4875 was still not in our control. The task of driving off Pakistanis from there was also assigned to 13 JAK Rif Rifleman Sanjay Kumar who didn't stop firing on the enemy even after getting hit by two bullets on his chest and arm. He first cleared one sangar and while striking the other, killed 3 enemy soldiers in face to face combat. The enemy fled away leaving its Universal Machine Gun and Subedar Sanjay Kumar used the same gun to rain bullets on the enemy and thus provided vital support in capturing the flat top area. He was awarded 'Param Vir Chakra' for this unprecedented valour and bravery. We captured the entire Point 4875 on 8th July 1999 and with this, we had gained control over all the important peaks in the sector. Our brave soldiers had demonstrated to the world that, whatever be the challenge, we were capable of aptly responding to the same. *India's victory over Point 4875 proved to be the last nail in the coffin of Pakistan.*

By 7th July 1999, the Kargil war had entered its decisive phase. On this very 7th July, we hoisted our victory flag over Point 4875 in Mushkoh valley, but a brave soldier Captain Vikram Batra had to lay down his life for the same. He was awarded 'Param Vir Chakra' for displaying his most conspicuous bravery.

We then went to Batra Transit Camp. This is an army camp that has been named after Captain Vikram Batra. This peak (4875) is now known as 'Batra Top' in his honour.

When Captain Vikram Batra's parents visited the war zone a few years after the war, the Indian Army had arranged their stay at this very camp. The Batra Top can also be seen clearly from this point. I got an opportunity in the year 2018 to meet Captain Batra's father Shri Girdhari Lal Batra and mother Smt Kanta Batra at his ancestral house at Palampur in Himachal Pradesh. I was also able to see Captain Batra's room where he spent his childhood. Now his memories are safely preserved there. I also had the pleasure of holding the 'Param Vir Chakra' that was awarded to him.

An important crossing on the Karnal bypass in Delhi has been named as 'Shaheed Captain Vikram Batra Chowk'. I have always been in favour of such actions. It's my request to install statues of the soldiers decorated with 'Param Vir Chakra' at the stations close to the places they hail from, and name any mail or express train originating from Delhi after them. I have been writing to the Ministry of Railways for the same. Let me explain this by example. Let's take the instance of Captain Manoj Kumar Pandey. There are eight trains that run between Delhi and Lucknow and have no specific names. Any one of these trains could be named as 'Shaheed Captain Manoj Pandey Express' and his statue should be installed at the main entry or exit point of Lucknow railway station with an inscription providing details of his bravery. Millions of youth who use the station or travel by that train named as 'Shaheed Captain Manoj Pandey Express' would definitely not only get acquainted with his life but also get inspired by his valour.

Every moment that I spent in Mushkoh valley during my trip in the year 2007 to Kargil is quite fresh in my mind even today. After visiting that place, it becomes difficult to believe that the same spot had witnessed such fierce fight sometime back. Mushkoh was much more beautiful than I had ever imagined.

Eventually, when India was driving out Pakistan from Tiger Hill on 4th July, Nawaz Sharif was at the door of the President of the United States, Bill Clinton with a plea for a ceasefire. India was obviously successful in bringing the situation under its complete control. Although the 4th of July is Independence Day for the United States, Clinton agreed for Nawaz's visit in view of the prevailing situation. But this was conditional—first, he would announce a ceasefire and second, he would deliver the same in a press conference. Nawaz Sharif had no option other than agreeing to the conditions, though he had already consulted Pervez Musharraf on the issue before leaving Pakistan.

Pakistan army always loses to us but still it always harbours evil plans. There is a saying that dog's tail can never be straightened; this aptly applies to Pakistan. Finally, a ceasefire was announced on 10th July 1999. This announcement could have been even made in the last week of June itself, had Nawaz Sharif got some valid reasons to save his face; he had of course made efforts for the same. Pakistan wanted to inflict maximum possible damage to India before leaving the ground. It comes to my mind quite often—had a ceasefire been declared in the last week of June, we could have prevented sacrifices of so many of our heroes. Alas, had that happened, Captain Vikram Batra and Captain Anuj Nayyar and a number of other brave soldiers would have been alive among us and would have been able to guide our young generation. Officially, this war started on 5th May 1999 and came to an end on 26th July 1999. The war went on for a total of 82 days. After declaration of the ceasefire, Pakistan started vacating the remaining posts; but this did not happen as smoothly as expected. Wherever they left, they planted landmines. The Indian Army had tough time clearing those posts. But what else could we expect from a country like Pakistan.

❑

10

Homecoming

We finished our breakfast at Kargil and left for Srinagar. On the way, we looked at the 'Tiger Hill' with all its grandeur again. Weather was quite pleasant that day too. We made a brief stopover at Zoji La Pass to have tea and click some photos and then headed for our destination, Srinagar. We took our lunch again at Sonmarg only. I had been thinking of having a *'darshan'* of Kheer Bhawani Mata for a long time, and the moment I expressed my desire to Bhat, he agreed to take us there. On reaching Ganderbal, he took the turn to the village of Tulmul, the site graced by Kheer Bhawani Mata. Kashmiri Pandits consider Kheer Bhawani Mata as their protective patron deity 'Kuldevi' and worship her with abundant faith. We noticed the army trucks bustling with activity there. Bhat informed that the place was quite prone to terrorist attacks. Even the temple premises were heavily guarded. Complying with those exhaustive security arrangements, we were taken through one gate after another, that too with intense security checks. We could sense the environment there was a bit tense.

We spent around an hour in the temple and then proceeded towards Srinagar. We asked Bhat to take a round of Dal Lake by road. It was around 5 in the evening when we were returning after some shopping near Hazaratbal. Corps from Central Reserve Police and Jammu & Kashmir Police could be seen in every nook and corner there. I was sitting in the front seat of Mahindra Scorpio. Suddenly, Bhat applied the brakes. I spotted some youth standing on the left side, all with their faces covered, only their eyes visible and nose opening clear for breathing. Until then, I had seen these so-called stone pelters on TV only. We all were stunned for a moment to see them in front of us. They were holding ball-shaped large stones, geared for specific use, in their hands. Bhat signalled to me to sit quiet and then made a gesture towards those boys also. And then, no idea how, they allowed our car to move. Some boys behind these youth were very leisurely playing cricket. All this happened within a span of just 60 seconds, but this incident shook me badly.

Thanks to the improving situation in the valley now, but anything could have happened that day. We bought some dry fruits and saffron for home use. Nowhere else can one find the kind of saffron that is available in Kashmir. The day was coming to an end. Bhat requested us to hurry a bit. The Railway Guest House of Badgam, where we had planned to stay overnight, was still around 10 km away. Our mobiles also were not receiving any signal. We all were feeling scared with a deathly silence inside the car. The car was speeding on that lonely unpaved road. Every five minutes, one of us would ask Bhat, "Brother, how long will it take to reach?" We felt as if our lives rested in Bhat's hands. Besides the frightening lonely terrain and the fear of stone-pelters, even the thought of somebody suddenly appearing in front of our car with a gun in his hand, making us come out and shooting us down point blank was keeping us constantly scared. In that very bafflement, we finally reached the Guest House and heaved a sigh of relief.

The next day, we reached Srinagar. The town was under curfew. Hardly any vehicle could be seen on the roads. Mostly forces of Army and CRPF could be seen around. We somehow managed to quickly have a glimpse of Srinagar station and rushed to the airport. We learnt there that the flight was rescheduled, that too a delay of 5 hours. That was quite a gloomy day. We somehow reached Delhi at 7pm.

After the Kargil war, the Army acquired all those weapons that were bitterly missed during the war. India now even boasts of Rafale, multiplying the power of our Air Force many times. Besides this, the Indian Government has also opened the doors for non-government and private companies to make arms in the country. This would not only curtail the production cycle time for weapons but also improve their quality.

My trips to the holy shine of Amarnath in the year 1999 and to Kargil in in the year 2007 and in year

2018 introduced me to a pristine spirit residing in my inner self that holds martyrs in high regard and is immensely devoted to the country. As such, these kinds of sentiments must be there in the heart of every Indian and that is what's expected, and in fact, we all do cherish such sentiments in our hearts. However, after visiting all these places and after witnessing the locales associated with the Kargil War, we did realise that all the heroes were well aware that the battles were going to be extremely fierce involving great risks with all kinds of possibilities, including considerably high risk of losing their lives. Despite that, ignoring their personal emotions and not even worrying about their near and dear ones, they all went to the battlefield and gladly lay down their lives for the pride of Bharat Mata. This sacrifice is too great to be ever repaid. The least we can do is to treasure the stories of the bravery, courage and sacrifice of those martyrs in our memory for always and keep remembering them and making our coming generations aware of the same.

Jai Hind!

❑

11

Gallantry Award Winners of Kargil War

Param Vir Chakra

1. Lt Manoj Kumar Pandey, 1/11 Gorkha Rifles (Posthumous).
2. Captain Vikram Batra, 13 Jammu & Kashmir Rifles (Posthumous).
3. Rifleman Sanjay Kumar, 13 Jammu & Kashmir Rifles.
4. Grenadier Yogendra Singh Yadav, 18 Grenadiers.

Maha Vir Chakra

1. Major Sonam Wangchuk, Ladakh Scouts (Indus Wing).
2. Major Vivek Gupta, 2 Rajputana Rifles (Posthumous).
3. Major Rajesh Singh Adhikari, 18 Grenadiers (Posthumous).

4. Major Padmapani Acharya, 2 Rajputana Rifles (Posthumous).
5. Captain Anuj Nayyar, 17 Jat Regiment (Posthumous).
6. Captain Neikezhakuo Kenguruse, 2 Rajputana Rifles (Posthumous).
7. Lt Keishing Clifford Nongrum, 12 Jammu & Kashmir Rifles L.I. (Posthumous).
8. Lt Balwan Singh, 18 Grenadiers.
9. Naik Digendra Kumar, 2 Rajputana Rifles.

Vir Chakra

1. Col Umesh Singh Bawa, 17 Jat Regiment.
2. Col Lalit Rai, 1/11 Gorkha Regiment.
3. Col M. B. Ravindranath, 2 Rajputana Rifles.
4. Lt Col. R. Vishwanathan, 18 Grenadiers (Posthumous).
5. Lt Col Yogesh Kumar Joshi, 13 Jammu & Kashmir Rifles.
6. Major Vijay Bhaskar, 13 Jammu & Kashmir Rifles.
7. Major Deepak Rampal, 17 Jat Regiment.
8. Major Vikash Vohra, 13 Jammu & Kashmir Rifles.
9. Major Amarinder Singh Kasana, 47 F.D. Regiment.

10. Major Rajesh Shah, 18 Garhwal Rifles.
11. Major Mohit Saxena, 2 Rajputana Rifles.
12. Major S, Sarvanan, 1 Bihar (Posthumous).
13. Captain Shyamal Sinha, 27 Rajputana Rifles.
14. Captain Amol Kalia, 12 Jammu & Kashmir Light Infantry (Posthumous).
15. Captain Sachin Annarao Nimbalkar, 18 Grenadiers.
16. Captain Sanjiv Singh, ASC, 13 Jammu & Kashmir Rifles.
17. Captain Haneefuddin, 11 Rajputana Rifles (Posthumous).
18. Captain Sumit Roy, 18 garhwal Rifles (Posthumous).
19. Captain Vijyant Thapar, 2 Rajputana Rifles (Posthumous).
20. Captain Maridhodhan Vitil Suraj, 18 Garhwal Rifles.
21. Captain Jintu Gogoi, 17 Garhwal Rifles (Posthumous).
22. Captain R. Jery Premraj, 158 Med. (Posthumous).
23. Subedar Chhering Stobdan, Ladakh Scouts (IW).
24. Subedar Bahadur Singh, 12 Jammu & Kashmir Rifles, Light Infantry (Posthumous).

25. Subedar Lobsang Chodak, Ladakh Scouts (IW) (Posthumous).
26. Subedar Randhir Singh, 18 Grenadiers (Posthumous).
27. Subedar Bhanwar Lal, 2 Rajputana Rifles (Posthumous).
28. Subedar Rahgunath Singh, 13 Jammu & Kashmir Rifles.
29. Naib Subedar Mangej Singh, 11 Rajputana Rifles (Posthumous).
30. N. C. Subedar Karnail Singh, 8 Sikh (Posthumous).
31. C.H.M. Yashveer Singh, 2 Rajputana Rifles (Posthumous).
32. Havildar Udham Singh, 18 Grenadiers (Posthumous).
33. Havildar Madan Lal, 18 Grenadiers (Posthumous).
34. Havildar Sultan Singh Narvariya, 2 Rajputana Rifles (Posthumous).
35. Havildar Kumar Singh, 17 Jat Regiment (Posthumous).
36. Havildar S.I.S. Tam Gill, 8 Jat Regiment (Posthumous).
37. Havildar Joginder Singh, Kumaon, 27 Rajput.

38. Havildar Tsewang Rigzin, Ladakh Scouts (IW) (Posthumous).

39. L./Havildar Ram Kumar, 18 Grenadiers (Posthumous).

40. Naik Kashmir Singh, 18 Garhwal Rifles (Posthumous).

41. N.K. Ganesh Prasad Yadav, 1 Bihar (Posthumous).

42. Naik Dev Prakash, 13 Jammu & Kashmir Rifles.

43. Lance Naik G. H. Mohd Khan, 12 Jammu & Kashmir Rifles, Light Infantry (Posthumous).

44. Lance Naik Khusiman Gurung, 1 Naga.

45. Sepoy Satpal Singh, 8 Sikh.

46. Sepoy Sering Dorje, Ladakh Scouts (IW).

47. Sepoy K. Ashuli, 1 Naga (Posthumous).

48. REN Jairan Singh, 2 Rajputana Rifles.

49. Rifleman Anusuya Prasad, 8 Garhwal Rifles (Posthumous).

50. Rifleman Kuldip Singh, 18 Garhwal Rifles (Posthumous).

51. Rifleman Shyam Singh, 13 Jammu & Kashmir Rifles (Posthumous).

52. Rifleman Mehar Singh, 13 Jammu & Kashmir Rifles.
53. GNR Sanjiv Gopal Pillay ARTY, 4 F.D. R.E.G.T. (Posthumous).
54. Wing Commander Anil Kumar Sinha, (16074) Flying Pilot.
55. Sqn Ldr Ajay Ahuja, (17864) Flying Pilot (Posthumous).

Sarvottam Yudh Seva Medal

1. Air Marshal Vinod Patani, P.V.S.M., A.V.S.M., V.R.C. (6125) Flying Pilot.

Uttam Yudh Seva Medal

1. Lt General Kishan Pal, P.V.S.M., V.S.M., Infantry.
2. Major General Mohinder Puri, Infantry.
3. Brigadier Prakash Chand Katoch, S., C. Infantry.
4. Brigadier Amarnath Aul, Infantry.
5. AVM Satinder Singh Dhillon, A.V.S.M., V.S.M. (7980) Aviation Engineering (Technical).
6. AVM Jaganandan Kumar Pathania, A.V.S.M., V.S.M. (8053) Administration.
7. AVM Narayan Menon, A.V.S.M. (9005) Flying Pilot.

Yudh Seva Medal

1. Brigadier Lakhvinder Singh, Artillery.
2. Brigadier Ramesh Kumar Kakkad, Infantry.
3. G.O. Captain Mathews Kurrhi Kombil Joseph (13393) Flying Pilot.
4. G.O. Captain Arvind Ramchandra Oak, (14103) Flying Pilot.
5. Wing Commander Sunderraman Neelakantan, V.M. (15184) Flying Pilot.
6. Wing Commander Birendra Singh Dhanoa, V.M. (15405) Flying Pilot.
7. Wing Commander Sandip Sood, (15685) Flying Pilot.
8. Wing Commander Sandip Chhabra (16032) Flying Pilot.

Bar to Sena Medal (Gallantry)

1. Col Samir Kumar Chakravorty, SC, SM, 18 Garhwal Rifles.

Sena Medal (Gallantry)

1. Col Devendra Singh Yadav, Sena AVN 663 R & O SQN.
2. Col Alok Deb, ARTY, 197 FD Regiment.
3. Col Prabhat Ranjan, ARTY, 108 Med Regiment.

4. Lt Col Girish Kumar Mendiratta, ARTY, 1889 Light Regiment.
5. Major Suresh Kumar Joshi, 18 Garhwal Rifles.
6. Major Ambrose Xavier Amalraj, ARTY, 108 Med Regiment.
7. Major Ravindra Singh, 8 Sikh.
8. Major Gurjeet Singh, Punjab, 5 Vikas.
9. Major Gurpreet Singh, 13 Jammu & Kashmir Rifles.
10. Major Amitabh Roy, ARTY, 8 Sikh.
11. Major Navdeep Singh Cheema, 27 Rajput.
12. Major Ajay Singh Jasrotia, 13 Jammu & Kashmir Rifles (Posthumous).
13. Major Joy Dasgupta, 18 Grenadiers.
14. Captain Harbir Singh, Sikh L.I., 5 Vikas.
15. Captain Ganesh Bhatt, 1889 Light Regiment.
16. Captain Kamath Prashant Narayan, 1889 LT Regiment.
17. Captain Mridul Kumar Singh, ARTY, 197 FD Regiment.
18. Captain P. V. Vikram. ARTY, 141 FD Regiment (Posthumous).
19. Captain Naveen Anaberu Nagappa, EME 13 Jammu & Kashmir Rifles.

20. Captain Saju Cherian, ARTY, 307 Med Regiment.

21. Captain Amit Sharma, ARTY, 197 FD REGT.

22. Captain Somnath Basu, AMC, 408 FD AMB.

23. Sanjay Barshiliya, ARTY, 286 Med Regiment.

24. Lt Praveen Tomar, ASC, 2 Rajputana Rifles.

25. Lt Rakesh Kumar Sehravat, 8 Sikh.

26. Lt Kanda Bhattacharya, AOC, 8 Sikh (Posthumous).

27. Subedar A. Heni MAO, 1 Naga.

28. Subedar Sumer Singh rathore, 2 Rajputana Rifles (Posthumous).

29. Subedar Joginder Singh, 8 Sikh (Posthumous).

30. Subedar Surendra Singh, 18 Garhwal Rifles.

31. Subedar Romesh Chand, 13 Jammu & Kashmir Rifles.

32. Naib Subedar Chanda Jat, 18 Grenadiers (Posthumous).

33. Naib Subedar Lal Singh, 18 Grenadiers (Posthumous).

34. Naib Subedar Sunayak Singh, 2 Rajputana Rifles.

35. Naik Subedar Tundup Dorje, Ladakh Scouts (IW).
36. Havildar Sribhagwan, 2 Rajputana Rifles.
37. Havildar Ranbir Singh, 2 Rajputana Rifles.
38. Havildar Sarman Singh Senga, 2 Rajputana Rifles (Posthumous).
39. Havildar Hari Om, 17 Jat regiment (Posthumous).
40. Havildar Gulam Kadir, Ladakh Scouts (IW).
41. Havildar Tam Bahadur Chhetri, 1 Naga (Posthumous).
42. L./Havildar Ramesh Chandra, 18 Grenadiers.
43. Naik Nirmal Singh Yadav, 18 Grenadiers.
44. Naik Samunder Singh, 18 Grenadiers (Posthumous).
45. Naik Ravi Kiran Singh, 18 Grenadiers (Posthumous).
46. Naik Karanbeer, 2 Rajputana Rifles.
47. Naik Balwan Singh, 17 Jat Regiment (Posthumous).
48. Naik Bahadur Singh, 8 Sikh (Posthumous).
49. Naik Ranjeet Singh, 8 Sikh (Posthumous).
50. Naik Jagat Singh, 18 Garhwal Rifles (Posthumous).

51. Naik Tashi Noorbu, Ladakh Scouts (IW).
52. Naik Mohan Lal, 13 Jammu & Kashmir Rifles.
53. Naik Swarn Singh, 13 Jammu & Kashmir Rifles.
54. Lance Naik Rajendra Kumar Yadav, 18 Grenadiers (Posthumous).
55. Lance Naik Shakti Singh, 18 Grenadiers.
56. Lance Naik Narayan Singh, 2 Rajputana Rifles.
57. Lance Naik Bhagwan Singh, 17 Rajput (Posthumous).
58. Lance Naik Kishan Singh, 18 Garhwal Rifles
59. Lance Naik Surman Singh, 18 Garhwal Rifles (Posthumous).
60. Lance Naik Sarwan Singh, 13 Jammu & Kashmir Rifles.
61. Lance Naik Kaushal Kumar Sharma, 13 Jammu & Kashmir Rifles.
62. Lance Naik Harish Pal, 13 Jammu & Kashmir Rifles (Posthumous).
63. Sepoy Bhanwar Singh Bharat, 27 Rajput (Posthumous).
64. Sepoy Surendra, 17 Jat Regiment (Posthumous).
65. Sepoy Puna Ram, 17 Jat Regiment.

66. Sepoy Major Singh, 8 Sikh (Posthumous).
67. Rifleman Narpal Singh, 18 Garhwal Rifles (Posthumous).
68. Rifleman Dabal Singh, 18 Garhwal Rifles (Posthumous).
69. Rifleman Natinder Singh,13 Jammu & Kashmir Rifles.
70. Rifleman Ajay Pathania,13 Jammu & Kashmir Rifles.
71. Rifleman Sunil Kuamr ,13 Jammu & Kashmir Rifles.
72. Rifleman Keval Kumar,13 Jammu & Kashmir Rifles.
73. Grenadier Munish Kumar, 18 Grenadiers (Posthumous).
74. Grenadier Kalyan Singh, 18 Grenadiers.
75. Grenadier Praveen Kumar, 18 Grenadiers (Posthumous).
76. Grenadier Raj Kumar, 18 Grenadiers (Posthumous).
77. Grenadier Udaybhan Singh, 18 Grenadiers (Posthumous).
78. Grenadier Dalip Singh, 18 Grenadiers
79. Grenadier Jagdish Prasad Gupta, 286 Med Regiment.
80. SPR M. Jaiveju, 2 Eng. RGT (Posthumous).

81. Signalman Vinod Kumar, 8 MDSR (Posthumous).
82. Company Havildar Chhombe, 5 Vikas.
83. Sahayak Havildar Tashi Phonsok, 5 Vikas.

Vayu Sena Medal (Gallantry)

1. Group Captain Satish Pal Singh, (13770) Flying Pilot.
2. Wing Commander Raghunath Nambiar, (16378) Flying Pilot.
3. Sqn Ldr Rajiv Pundir, (17143) Flying Pilot (Posthumous).
4. Sqn Ldr Mohan Rao, (17343) Flying Pilot.
5. Sqn Ldr Vishwas Gaud, (17361) Flying Pilot.
6. Sqn Ldr Sanjay Bhatnagar, (17363) Flying Pilot.
7. Sqn Ldr Gurcharan Singh Bedi, (17448) Flying Pilot.
8. Sqn Ldr Dilip Kumar Patnaik, (17464) Flying Pilot.
9. Sqn Ldr Ajay Prakash Srivastava, YSM (17471) Flying Pilot.
10. Sqn Ldr Alok Chaudhary, (18271) Flying Pilot.
11. Sqn Ldr Narendra Singh Varma, (18298) Flying Pilot.

12. Sqn Ldr Amanjit Singh Heer, (19521) Flying Pilot.
13. Sqn Ldr Nitish Kumar, (19898) Flying Pilot.
14. Sqn Ldr Harendra Pal Singh, (20477) Flying Pilot.
15. Flt Lt Sriped Tokakar, (21815) Flying Pilot.
16. Flt Lt Rajesh Walia, (21858) Flying Pilot.
17. Flt Lt Ashish Gupta, (22121) Flying Pilot.
18. Flt Lt Subramanian Muhilan, (22739) Flying Pilot (Posthumous).
19. Flt Lt Gaurav Chhibbar, (22926) Flying Pilot (Posthumous).
20. Flt Lt Kambampati Nachiketa, (22930) Flying Pilot.
21. Flying Officer Rajpal Singh Dhaliwal, (23535) Flying Pilot.
22. W.O. Krishna Singh Dhillon, Flying Engineer.
23. SGT Pasad Pila Venkat Narayan Ravi, Flight Gunner (Posthumous).
24. SGT Sahu Taj Kishore, Flight Engineer (Posthumous).

❑

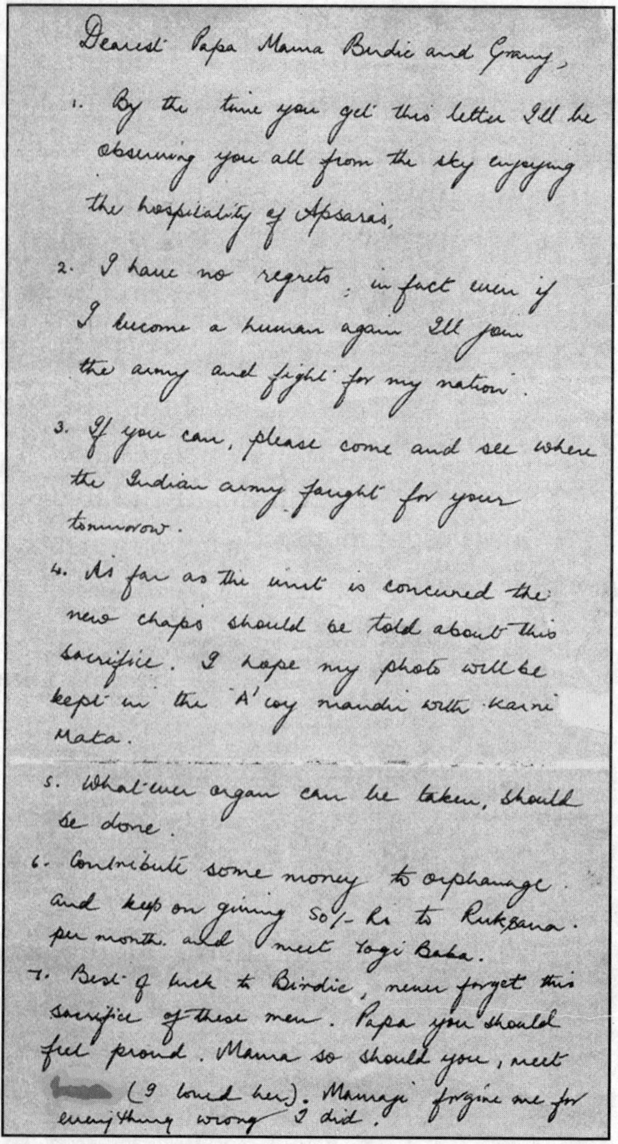

Dearest Papa Mama Birdie and Granny,

1. By the time you get this letter I'll be observing you all from the sky enjoying the hospitality of Apsaras.

2. I have no regrets; in fact even if I become a human again I'll join the army and fight for my nation.

3. If you can, please come and see where the Indian army fought for your tommorow.

4. As far as the unit is concerned the new chaps should be told about this sacrifice. I hope my photo will be kept in the 'A' coy mandir with Karni Mata.

5. What ever organ can be taken, should be done.

6. Contribute some money to orphanage and keep on giving 50/- Rs to Rukhsana per month and meet Yogi Baba.

7. Best of luck to Birdie, never forget this sacrifice of these men. Papa you should feel proud. Mama so should you, meet [illegible] (I loved her). Mamaji forgive me for everything wrong I did.

Last letter of Capt. Vijyant Thapar to his father.

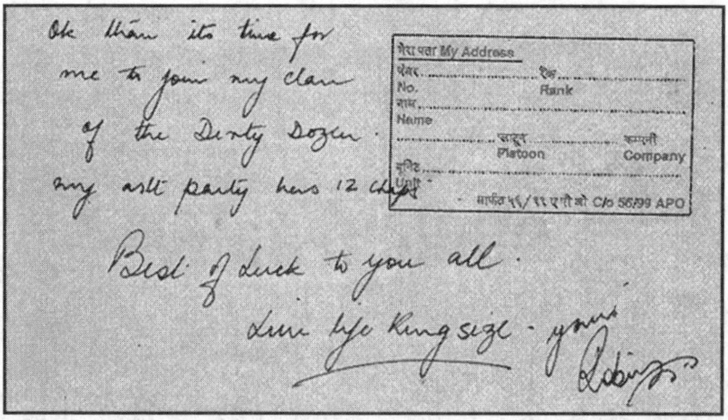

Ok then its time for
me to join my clan
of the Dirty Dozen.
my asslt party has 12 chaps

Best of luck to you all.
Live life king size - yours
Robin

मेरा पता My Address
No. Rank
Name
Platoon Company
Unit
C/o 56/99 APO

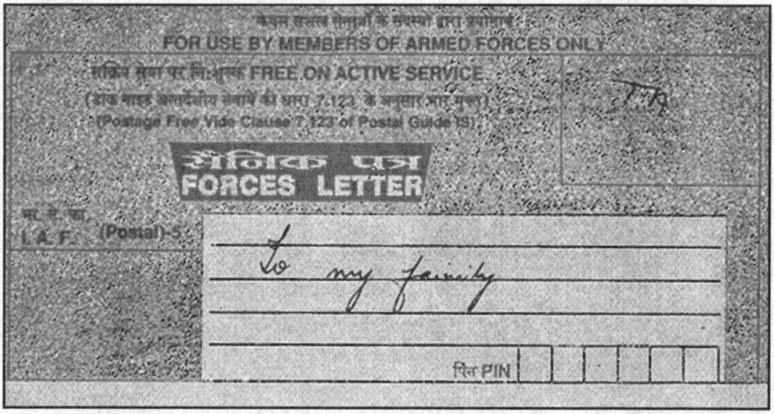

FOR USE BY MEMBERS OF ARMED FORCES ONLY
FREE ON ACTIVE SERVICE
(Postage Free Vide Clause 7.123 of Postal Guide IS)
सैनिक पत्र
FORCES LETTER
I. A. F. (Postal)-5
to my family
पिन PIN

Last letter of Capt. Vijyant Thapar to his father.

Bibliography

- *Dateline Kargil*—By Gaurav C. Sawant
- *Kargil: Turning the Tide*—By Lt. Gen. Mohinder Puri
- *Kargil: From Surprise to Victory*— By General V.P. Malik
- *A Ridge Too Far*—By Captain Amarinder Singh
- *A Soldier's Diary: Kargil the Inside Story*—By Harinder Baweja
- *Vijyant at Kargil: The Life of a Kargil War Hero*—By Col. V.N. Thapar & Neha Dwivedi
- *Kargil untold stories from the war*—By Rachna Bisht Rawat
- *Kargil: The Heights of Bravery*—By Azad Singh Rathore
- *Letters from Kargil*—By Diksha Dwivedi
- *From Kargil to the Coup*—By Nasim Zehra
- *The Kargil Victory*—By Col. S.C. Tyagi
- *Despatches from Kargil*—By Srinjoy Chowdhury
- Articles—By Defence Services officers Institute.
- *Kargil Review Committee report.*

❑❑❑